This World Book Day 2021 book is
a gift from your local bookseller,
Katherine Rundell and Bloomsbury.
#ShareAStory

WORLD BOOK DAY

World Book Day's mission is to offer every child and young person the opportunity to read and love books by giving you the chance to have a book of your own.

To find out more, and get great recommendations on what to read next, visit **worldbookday.com**

World Book Day is a charity funded by publishers and booksellers in the UK and Ireland.

World Book Day is also made possible by generous sponsorship from National Book Tokens and support from authors and illustrators.

SKYSTEPPERS

KATHERINE RUNDELL

BLOOMSBURY
CHILDREN'S BOOKS
LONDON OXFORD NEW YORK NEW DELHI SYDNEY

BLOOMSBURY CHILDREN'S BOOKS
Bloomsbury Publishing Plc
50 Bedford Square, London WC1B 3DP, UK
29 Earlsfort Terrace, Dublin 2, Ireland

First published in Great Britain in 2021 by Bloomsbury Publishing Plc

A catalogue record for this book is available from the British Library

ISBN: 978-1-5266-3045-2

2 4 6 8 10 9 7 5 3 1

Typeset by Westchester Publishing Services

Printed and bound in Great Britain by CPI Group (UK) Ltd, Croydon CR0 4YY

To find out more about our authors and books visit www.bloomsbury.com
and sign up for our newsletters

For Theodora and Rainbow

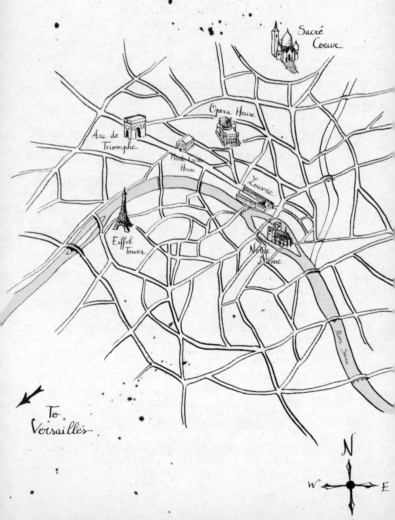

CHAPTER ONE

It was the evening of Matteo's eleventh birthday, and he was stealing a cucumber.

There were many ways in which it could have been fine, and only one in which it could have been a disaster. Unfortunately, as Matteo found, probabilities don't always play nice.

He had done it many times before. If the woman behind whom he was hiding had not moved – if the two policemen had not been bored, and looking for something to do – everything, for the rest of his life, might have been different. Instead, the woman twisted to pick up a cabbage, one of the policemen gave a sudden roar, and Matteo and the cucumber took off through the lamp-lit streets of Paris.

He was fast, and he knew how to move through a crowd. He dodged in front of one carriage, behind another, around a man on a bicycle, who yelled something which Matteo might, in less urgent moments, have carefully memorised for later use. He ducked under the belly of a vast horse – for a second, he thought about swinging up on to it and away, but the horse was attached to the rubbish cart, and it seemed impractical.

'Stop him! Stop that boy!' The policemen were gaining on him.

Matteo sprinted down the boulevard, holding the cucumber out in front of him like a dagger, and veered into a street called the Rue Gluck. The great Paris Opera was nearby, and that always attracted crowds – crowds, perhaps, that he could hide in.

A group of Belgian tourists, clad in rigorously serious shoes, stood looking up at the great wedding-cake of a building. He tried to merge into them, but there were no other children. Besides, Matteo felt his shoes looked insufficiently earnest. And at the far end of the road, there was another policeman: a lithe, sporting-looking man, fishing something out from between his teeth with the end of his penknife.

'No need to run!' called one policeman. 'He can't

escape!' The lithe officer stopped working on his teeth, and came striding down the street. There was no way out.

It took Matteo less than a second to decide. If there was no *out*, he would go *up*.

The Opera House might have been built to be climbed. Matteo had always felt rather scornful about the pillars and the carved figures and golden faces that adorned its sides. The designer of the building, he thought, must have had an addiction to winged nymphs. But they made it the perfect climbing wall.

He edged round the side, reached out and grasped the drainpipe. He yanked off his boots, shoved one in each pocket, set his toes behind the pipe, put the cucumber between his teeth, braced against the wall, and pushed himself upwards.

The pipe was exactly the right size for his two hands to wrap round. Clammy and breathless and shaking, he climbed; once he was high enough, he stretched sideways and transferred his weight to one of the carved angels. His palms were sweaty with fear; he tried to wipe one on his hair, but hair is no good for wiping. One hand on a goddess's foot, one in the mouth of a golden old man: pull, breathe. Someone gave a shout below – but he did not look down until he was within reach of the top.

The top of the building was a great copper dome, turned green with age, and on the centre of the dome stood a bronze statue of the Greek god Apollo. Matteo crouched behind the parapet, looking up at Apollo's behind, over which the sculptor had clearly taken considerable time, and tried to get his breath back.

He could hear the policemen calling to each other down below.

'Where'd he go? What happened?' The man took off his glasses and rubbed his eyes.

'He went up!'

'You're seeing things, Jean-Luc! It's getting dark.'

'I swear, he went up the statues. He put his foot in the mouth of the Angel of Lyric Drama – I saw it!'

The lithe policeman grunted. 'I don't fancy trying to explain that to the captain, I'm telling you. Think of the paperwork.'

'Ach, let's leave it!' said the older man. 'He was just a nuisance.'

It seemed impossibly good luck for someone whose luck had never run particularly lucky – good enough to

4

make up for the bad luck of being chased. There they were, walking away.

Matteo dusted down his hands and adjusted his clothes, sucked the blood off his arm where it had dragged against the brickwork, and stood up. He leaned over the gold-rimmed parapet and took in his surroundings.

It was a dizzying feeling. Matteo had climbed many trees before, but never a rooftop. His whole body was stuttering. The chase, he realised, had eaten him up: fear is exhausting, and even though he would not have admitted it to himself, he had been afraid. Matteo had no family, which meant he had nobody who would help him if he were caught.

He walked the whole surface of the roof. It was not, he thought, so bad up here. It was quieter – more private. The people in the street below all watched each other and passed judgement, even if just very fleetingly, on each other's everything – shoes, clothes, face, walk, money, power. Up here, nobody could see him. Up here, nobody could chase him.

He looked out over Paris. The lights flickering on made it look unfamiliar and alive. He had been born in Paris – at least, he supposed he had – and knew, as all Parisians do, that it was the greatest place on earth. Yet he had never really looked at it before now. Its streets twisted and wound round churches and great hotels and tiny cafes, and through it all the great River Seine, turning midnight-blue as the summer evening fell.

Beneath his feet, the orchestra struck up, and the opera began, vibrating through his shoes and all the way into his lungs. The music made him feel reckless. In the dark, he climbed up on to the ledge of the parapet and stood right at the edge, with his toes curled over the drop into nothing. He felt his stomach swoop in an entire cycle of his body: it was in his feet, skull, knees, chest. At one point it felt like it was possibly in his ears. It was terrifying, and electric.

He should really, he thought, go back down.

But up here it was like nothing else he'd ever felt – it was like being drunk on the air. Up here, high above the streets and the world that walks in them, even a child with a hole in his shoe could feel like a king. It was the perfect place for a birthday feast. He stuck a lit match into the cucumber in place of a candle, and sang, very softly, *Happy birthday to me*. And he decided to stay.

* * *

Some people are just born to be a little more skywards than the rest of us. Matteo was one of them.

He developed very strong opinions about brickwork: about those bricks which left space for hands, and the foolishness of those that did not. He developed passions for things he did not expect to have passions for – a good piece of metal guttering, for instance, that could take your weight, and window sills thick enough for you to land on and take off from. Ever since he was very small, Matteo's hands and feet had obeyed him more than other people's seemed to. He told this hand to grip on and not let go, and it did. His temper was not so easily his own: but his arms and legs, yes – most of the time.

Once it was dark, Matteo made his way across the streets of his city on the rooftops, clambering round chimney pots, jumping where it was possible to jump, sliding down and shinning up drainpipes, searching for food. The sliding down was easy; it was too fast to be very afraid. Climbing back up again required him to take hold of every inch of his imagination in both hands, squeezing it down so that it would not serve up thoughts about slipping and falling and dying.

Down at pavement level, stealing food had been grim,

grinding work. But these houses, the rich ones along the banks of the Seine; their window sills were like larders: they left out pies to cool, fruit to ripen. He stamped down, hard, on any guilt he felt. The beautiful kitchens were full of food, and, he told himself, they would probably be glad to give it to him, if he asked. Some of it, anyhow. Probably.

One week passed, and then two, and a third. Some nights it was very good. He lay on his back, on the curved dome of the Opera House roof, listening to the music. He discovered that he liked opera, which was, he thought, an enjoyably furious kind of music – rather as if all the stars in the sky had got angry and hurled themselves into your face all at once. On those nights, it felt like this could become a home.

But on other nights, the Opera House felt very large and empty, and he felt very small and empty, and his stomach would grow heavy and cold – and then he went, carefully, on hands and knees, over other rooftops. He would squat behind chimney stacks and stare in at families, at children, at people laughing and whispering and shouting and living alongside each other. Once, he found his hand stretching out towards them. He bit it, as punishment, and sat on it sternly. That was sentimental. He was not that. He was a rooftop boy now.

He discovered some families he liked more than others. There were rich families, with tables bending under the weight of fashionable dishes – mutton with cream, roast heron, fish jelly – where he only ever went at dinner-time, to smell it through the chimney. There were poor families, where the meals smelt of potato water, but the jokes tended to be better. Once, he dropped a dead plucked pigeon as an offering down one of the chimneys, but the family reacted disappointingly: more screaming, and less gratitude, than he'd expected.

On days when it rained, and the window sills were empty, he ate bread he kept stored in a tin, so old it was like trying to eat one of his own teeth. He slept curled in a corner of the Opera dome, in a den made of brown sacks stitched with pigeon feathers, and a blanket he had borrowed from a horse. His fingers grew calloused and tough. He spoke to nobody, smiled at nobody. He was safe, but he was also alone.

Except, it turned out, he was not.

CHAPTER TWO

Matteo was on top of an accountants' office at midnight, harvesting weathervanes. He had found that by snapping off the pointed end, he could bind it to a stick, and make very acceptable arrows. He had made a bow from a long piece of ash, and borrowed some string from a washing line strung in a narrow street in the Marais district. Now he pivoted, crouched low, and took aim.

A pigeon on the building opposite had come to roost on a chimney pot. It ruffled its feathers, closed its eyes: and Matteo let fly. The arrow shot through the air, and caught the pigeon in the heart. Matteo crowed with triumph. He was scrambling towards it when a ginger cat appeared, took the pigeon in its mouth, and leaped to the next rooftop.

Matteo gave a snort of fury. 'Hey! That's mine!' He had no intention of sharing his dinner. He started out after the cat, running crouched low on hands and feet; the moon was covered by cloud, and Matteo could only just see the slates under his bare toes.

The cat clearly believed in the law of finders keepers, and it was moving fast; it went down the entire length of a street, with Matteo close behind, hissing insults at it. It leaped on to the adjacent row of rooftops on the Rue de Ponthieu. Matteo hesitated. The roof opposite had a ledge as high as his knees, so he would have to make it over two metres and also clear the ledge. He took a run-up of three houses long. As he took off, he pushed with all his might at the thought that said, *This is how people die.* And he put, in its place, as loud as he could, something else. *Pain au chocolat!* he thought. *Butter!*

It worked, though only a little.

He landed, scraping a good portion of skin from his knee, and ran on. But the cat, its feet so sure against the tiles, ran faster, eyes shining in the blackness; then it made one final leap, and came to a halt.

Matteo stared into the darkness. As he did so, the moon broke free and he could see. He did not know exactly what he expected, but if he had been asked to describe exactly what he did *not* expect, it would have been this:

a large townhouse, crumbling with age, six storeys high, with a flat rooftop, and almost every inch of it packed with cats.

And through the cats, seemingly ignoring them, expecting them to part and scatter, moved a small figure – a child about his own size, wearing a fencing helmet and jabbing a fencing blade at the moonlight: stabbing, parrying, ducking and whirling.

Another boy, thought Matteo. *Up on the rooftop.* It seemed impossible. Another child who had discovered that it was possible to live up among the birds and storms and stars?

As he watched, the ginger cat approached the boy and laid the pigeon – *his* pigeon – at his feet. The child stroked the cat, balanced the pigeon on the edge of the chimney, and went back to stabbing at the air.

Matteo's astonishment was tinged with annoyance. He bristled. Matteo did not believe in theft, unless he was the one carrying it out. He jumped the metre between the rooftops and landed noiselessly – more so than he had intended. The boy, whose back was to him, did not hear.

Matteo cleared his throat. 'That's my pigeon, actually.'

The child leaped a full foot and twisted in the air,

letting out a noise between a yelp and a growl. 'What are you doing here?' he said. 'This is my rooftop!'

'Do you live up here?' asked Matteo.

'What if I do? Get away!'

'I'm not wanting your rooftop – I'm wanting my pigeon.'

'It's not yours.'

'I shot it.'

They both looked at the pigeon. It still had the arrow in it.

'Why should I believe that's your arrow?'

Matteo pointed at the other, identical arrow in his belt. They both looked at the weathervane-arrow in the pigeon, and at the one at Matteo's side.

'I mean, if this was a murder case, I'd be convicted.'

'I don't care.' The boy levelled his weapon at Matteo. 'Get off, or I'll make you.'

Matteo would not have considered a pigeon worth fighting for. The sky, after all, was full of them. But it was the principle of the thing, and Matteo had fierce principles, albeit ones of his own unique invention. He pulled the arrow from his belt, and lunged.

The fight was short. Matteo had grown up fighting; he

knew the details of it – it is best to strike hard and fast. But this boy knew it too. They circled each other, the cats parting before them like water. Matteo trod on a tail, and there was a yowl, and the boy growled again. He tried to get a jab in under the armpit, and the boy's weapon came up against his side, stinging like fire. He could see, now; it was a long, hand-whittled piece of wood, and set in the end was an iron nail as sharp as a dagger.

'Just … go …' gasped the boy, and lunged.

Matteo stepped backwards, and backwards again – he jabbed, ducked, but the other's weapon was longer, and it moved so fast that no matter what he did, the nail was always just inches from his chest. He stepped back again, and felt his heels edge back over nothingness – only the front half of his feet were on the slate. He gasped, realigned his centre, held steady, breathed.

Abruptly the boy dropped the weapon. 'Get away from the edge!'

'What?' Matteo stayed where he was, half on and half off. 'I thought you were trying to kill me? Do you not want to make up your mind?'

'Do it! Now! I'll give you the pigeon. Even though I was winning. Do it!'

Matteo shrugged. He stepped forward, both feet safely on hard slate.

'More. Come properly back to the middle.'

Matteo followed the boy back to the chimney pots.

'Better.' And the child pulled the helmet off.

Dark hair fell down her back. Her eyes were large and turned up a little at the edges, and she had a mole just above a wide, generous mouth.

'Oh!' he said. 'You're –' but she gave him a look of such ferocity that it seemed unwise to say, 'a girl!' He switched: '… afraid of edges?'

'So?'

'So nothing!' He shifted away, just in case the rapier was about to appear again. 'I only wondered.'

'I hate heights, OK?'

'What?' Matteo blinked so hard that both of his eyes felt bruised. 'It's just … you're living on a *rooftop*.'

'I know!'

'I mean – I don't want to be rude, but that seems an odd life decision.'

'Look – it's fine if I don't go near the edge, but if I do, my legs turn to sort of … juice.'

'You weren't near the edge! I was.'

'I don't know why, but that's just as bad.' She picked up the pigeon and lobbed it at Matteo, who caught it and put it in his jacket pocket. 'You can go now.'

But Matteo found himself unwilling to leave. He crossed to one of the chimney stacks and sat down defiantly. One of the cats climbed into his lap. Up close, he could see the fencing mask was made from cardboard and chicken wire. The girl lifted her home-made rapier, and for a moment he wondered if she was going to attack him again, but instead she tucked it neatly between the chimney pots and sat down.

'I *can* climb down and back up again.' She took a basin of water from behind the chimney, and washed her hands. They were soft and brown and long-fingered, and looked nimble. 'But it makes my chest hot, and sometimes I do a tiny bit of vomit in my mouth.'

'Then … how do you get food?'

'The cats bring it to me, most nights. Look! Over there.'

A black cat approached over the rooftops. It was missing half an ear and two toes, and did not look friendly. It carried an entire mackerel in its mouth.

'Thank you, Mirabeau.' She stood, and curtsied gravely to the cat. 'That is very generous of you.' She glanced at

Matteo, to check that he wasn't laughing. He made sure his face was expressionless. 'They like a bit of ceremony, the cats. They feel it's what they deserve.'

She took a knife from her pocket and gutted the fish. The cats nearest her snatched the guts and made off with them. 'If you bow to a cat for long enough, they'll do almost anything in return. That's where people have been going wrong. See! It's half past midnight. That's when they come.'

Matteo looked to where she was pointing – and saw, over the rooftops, shadows moving towards them. A scruffy creature with huge eyes and a whirling tail reached them first, dragging in its mouth a half-eaten squirrel. It did not look recently dead.

The girl sighed. 'You can only train them so far – they know to bring food, but they haven't learned that I don't eat squirrel.'

The cat dropped the squirrel in front of Matteo.

'You need to bow,' she said.

Matteo did not bow to anyone, cats included. He saluted instead.

'Now tell it your name.'

'It's a cat.'

She grinned. 'Have you no manners?'

He sighed. 'I'm Matteo, Monsieur Cat.'

'Good,' said the girl. 'I'm Mercédès.'

'Mercédès, then – if you hate being up high – why come up here? Are you hiding from someone? Are you on the run?'

She shook her head. 'I'm guarding.' She checked the fish for cat-teeth marks. 'We'll smoke the fish.'

She took what looked like a tiny string hammock from a pile of neatly folded scraps of cloth. She wrapped the fish in it, and lowered it down the smoking chimney. 'Listen! There! She's just starting! That's what I'm guarding.'

From the chimney, soft, just distinguishable, came a voice. It was singing, accompanied by a violin. It was not a good voice, technically – it was old, and it wavered on the high notes – but it had the richness of a voice that had, once, been a thing to make you drop to your knees. It made the hair on Matteo's arms stand up. He scowled at his arms and rubbed them. Then the voice jolted over a high note, and the violin twanged, and rich laughter broke out below.

'That's Madame Clotilde Valmy. She was a great opera star. She lives with Madame Églantine in this house.

Églantine is the violinist. They're what I'm here to look after.'

'Why do you care about them? Are they your aunts or something?'

'No! When I was very tiny, my mother heard Clotilde sing in a concert. She said: if she'd heard that every day, she might have been happy. It's the only thing I remember her loving, except me. So you see, I need to protect them.'

Matteo frowned. 'How long have you been up here?'

'Since before winter. I wasn't protecting them at first. My great-aunt, who I lived with – she died last November, and I had nobody. I thought – I might as well live some-where that I can hear the thing my mama loved. Mama was from Morocco, by the sea. She brought me to Paris when I was four, the year before she died. Mama missed the sound of the water. She said Clotilde Valmy sang like the waves.'

Matteo had never heard the sea, but he secretly thought it was unlikely that it sounded like anyone singing. Surely someone would have mentioned it. But he said nothing. His talent was for watching, for hearing, for noticing things and for storing them in piles in the back of his mind – and he had learned long ago that if you let people talk without interrupting, they end by telling you their secrets.

'But what are you guarding them *from*?' he asked.

'From a man: a money-man. A bully, a criminal, a thug: Henri Danglars,' Mercédès said, and spat. 'Clotilde's father died very old, and he left some debts. Danglars came and said he could help them, but he's just a snake in a suit. He's been threatening to throw them out into the street unless they pay him the money he says they owe.'

'So they're poor?' It was a grand house, he thought, for people with huge debts.

Mercédès nodded. 'They just have the attic apartment. Clotilde's grandmother was a cook for the man who used to own the house. He was a count – the Count of Monty Something – and he left the apartment to her. It's all they've got. But the last time Danglars came, he said it was a final warning.' Lightly she touched the sharp tip of her weapon. 'It's why I train. To be ready to help them. I'm their guardian angel. Except I eat their food. Which I think guardian angels don't do.'

Matteo did not know what good a wooden stick with a nail would be against a debt collector, but he only said, 'Do they know you're up here?'

'I don't think so – but they must know that there's *something* up here, because they leave food out on the window sills. I never take more than the cats would be able to – and I make sure it doesn't look too neat.'

It seemed strange to Matteo. But he had lived long enough and hard enough to know that strange things, if you dig down right into them, are often not so very strange at all. And strangeness, either way, was not something he was afraid of.

The smell of the fish from the chimney was stronger now, and the cats were clustering round. There were tortoiseshell cats as large as small tigers, and hordes of scrambling, scrapping kittens – Matteo gave up counting after twenty-five – many of them were small enough to fit in the palm of your hand. The mewing was as loud as his orchestra down at the Opera.

Mercédès fished the mackerel out of the chimney. 'It's like having my very own smokehouse. And it only tastes very slightly disgusting.' She dropped the fish on to a piece of paper. 'That's another thing they leave out on the window sills: parchment scraps, old bills. The Count left piles and piles of papers, so they've been tearing them up and putting them out here: I think they imagine the crows will use it for their nests.' She sliced the fish neatly in two, and handed one half to Matteo.

'What about you? Why are you up here?'

Matteo shrugged. He was happy to ask questions, not to answer them. 'It's better, for me.' The fish was warming, and tasted of chimney dust and the sea. 'Did you know, it's illegal to be homeless in France? Up here, nobody can tell me I'm illegal. Nobody can tell me *anything*. I am just me.'

He swallowed the fish in three burning-hot-outside, slightly-raw-inside mouthfuls, and stood. A kitten tried to bite his ankle, and he gently shook it off. 'I'm going.'

'Come back sometime,' said the girl. 'It's quite nice talking to someone who isn't a cat.'

CHAPTER THREE

Matteo put off going back. Other people were dangerous, even ones with large brown eyes and wonky expressive eyebrows.

He spent a week exploring the rooftops along the River Seine instead. He discovered a rooftop where mushrooms grew in the gutter, which, fried on a hammered-flat tin can, tasted of steak (if you squinted with your taste buds). The mushroom rooftop belonged to an old French professor, a man so alarmingly learned that he took half an hour to finish a single sentence. Matteo would sit on the chimney pot and listen: 'What a gorgeous day for our lecture! Are you ready, gentlemen? Then – but that's rather a fascinating word, *gorgeous*, don't you think? It comes from the Old French, *gorgias*, meaning an ornament worn around the neck – which itself arises from the medieval word for throat, *gargouille* – which is also where the *gargoyle* got its name … Rather ironic, no, that *gorgeous* and *gargoyle* are related? But forgive me, I'm getting distracted …' Matteo liked him, and liked the butter he left out on the window sill.

But after a week, Matteo found himself moving as soon as it grew dark, fake-casually, towards the west. It was stormy: one of those summer storms that lights up the sky, and he made his way slowly over the rooftops, chewing at the tail end of a loaf of bread and wiping the rain out of his eyes. He told himself that he was just going for an evening walk; his legs, though, thought otherwise, and led him along the roofs of the Rue Bayard towards the vast, tumbledown house. A white cat padded behind him, carrying half a shrew in its mouth. Matteo knew where it was going.

Mercédès was wearing what looked like a raincoat made of cats: they sat on her shoulders and stretched across her chest, guarding her from the downpour. They all looked furious.

He made the jump to her rooftop, slippery in the wet, and was about to speak when she jerked her arm to stop him, sending two cats flying.

'Shh! Come! Listen!' She was leaning over the chimney

pot. Her ears were twitching. 'It's him! The man who's been threatening them. Monsieur Danglars!'

Matteo leaned in next to her, a cat's ear in his eye. The voice that filtered up the chimney was harsh, and blunt as a spade on metal.

'The debt is due *tonight*. My rights in the matter are clear. This apartment is now mine.'

There was a choked sob.

'Please! We just need a few more days, and we can come up with a payment.'

'Time is a luxury, Madame. It is not one you can afford.'

Then the voices moved away and became indistinct. Matteo looked up and saw Mercédès' face, twisted with worry.

'This man, Danglars! He keeps coming. He terrifies them!'

'But … I don't understand – Why does he say the apartment is his?'

'You know that there was a debt, from Clotilde's father? Well, one day Danglars came to the door and said he would lend them the money to clear the debt – but only if they promised that if they couldn't repay within a year, they would give him their apartment as payment. But he cheated them! He charged them far, far more money than they borrowed in the first place – it's called *interest*, and he says they have to pay him back 1,509 per cent per year of what they borrowed – and every week the debt got huger and huger. It's fifteen times as big now as it used to be: they'll never be able to repay it.'

'*Fifteen*? Is that legal?'

'Apparently. I don't know. Do I look like a banker?'

She did not look like a banker. She was wearing a Siamese cat as a hat.

'But that's vile!' said Matteo.

Before Mercédès could answer, there was the sound of a door slamming, and a terrible silence fell on the murmuring chimney voices. Mercédès turned to Matteo, her eyes huge and panicked. 'What's he done? What's he done to them?'

Matteo crossed to peer over into the street. The front door opened, and two old women came slowly out. One was tall and broad, and her grey hair, cut short and curled, stood up in little tufts at the back where she had slept restlessly on it.

'That's Madame Églantine!' whispered Mercédès next to him.

The other was smaller and thinner, her back as straight as a door jamb. She wore a white plait down her back, so long its tip touched the puddles on the pavement. The rain had stopped, but it had left a vicious chill in the air.

'That's Madame Clotilde! That's her! She was once the most famous singer in all Paris!'

The two old women stood, bewildered, looking about them. Each carried a suitcase, and Églantine held a violin case. Clotilde clutched a cloth bag from which protruded the handles of two saucepans. Their hands, veined with purple, did not look strong enough for their burdens. The skin looked papery thin, as if it would tear in two.

They hesitated in the doorway of what, just moments ago, had been their own home. A single tear ran down Églantine's nose. Clotilde opened her mouth to speak, and then clamped it tight shut, as if to stop a cry escaping into the night air. A passing gentleman in a top hat, alarmed, stepped into the street to avoid them.

'Come, Egg,' said Clotilde. 'Come, we'll go and—'

'Come *where*, Tilde? Where are we to go?' And her voice cracked, and the tears ran down her cheeks and splashed on to her suitcase. 'Where?' And she cried out, '*Where?*'

A woman got out of a shining four-horse carriage across the road, and grimaced at the sight of them.

Matteo felt a hot spurt of shame and rage rise in him. He had the sudden conviction that he too had lived through a moment like this one, in a different place, so long ago he didn't truly remember it – only felt it in his guts and lungs and skin. He wanted to kill the man who had done it to them.

Mercédès turned to Matteo. Tears were in her eyes, and her voice was high. 'Do something!'

'Me? What can I do?'

'Something! Come up with something! We have to!'

But Clotilde and Églantine had picked up their suit-cases and were walking, slowly and painfully, into the night, which opened its mouth wide to receive them.

CHAPTER FOUR

They sat in silence, the two of them, as the sky grew darker. Matteo bit down on his knee, and tried to force the misery in his chest to recede. It impolitely refused to do so.

Then from the chimney pot there came a sudden cacophony of noise – banging and crashing, and a grunt of fury. Both children jumped. Matteo could make out the sound of drawers slamming, and what sounded like crockery hitting the floor.

'What's he doing?' cried Mercédès. 'Why is he destroying their home?'

'I'm going to look in the window,' said Matteo.

'Wait!'

'I won't let him see me!'

'No – I meant, I'm coming too.'

Matteo didn't argue. Carefully, mouse-quietly, they

clambered down the drainpipe, Mercédès first, then Matteo. Clutching on to it, braced against the wall, they peered in the window.

The room was small, painted a rich yellow, and crowded with books. By the light of an oil lamp, Danglars moved through it. He seized each individual book, shook it by the spine, then threw it into a pile on the floor. Drawers had been pulled out of chests, and the contents dumped on the floor.

Mercédès turned to Matteo. She spoke barely above a breath. 'Danglars isn't destroying the apartment. He's *searching* it.'

Back on the rooftop, they sat staring at each other in bewilderment.

'Could they have left money in the books?' said Matteo. 'Is that what he's searching for?'

'They don't *have* any money! They have nothing worth anything – only Madame Églantine's violin. And now they're on the street, and it's dark, and they didn't even have proper clothes.' Her voice shook.

Matteo stood up. He knew it is easier not to despair

when your hands and feet are warm. 'Shall we light a fire? It's late enough now.'

She nodded and shivered, and the remaining cats shivered with her. 'If we do it next to the chimney pots, nobody will know the smoke isn't from inside.'

Behind the chimney pots there was a sack, and in it a heaping of mostly dry paper scraps. 'Kindling,' said Mercédès. 'They were left on the window sill.'

There was a heap of wood too, and though it was damp, together they were able to light the fire with only a small number of burned fingers.

They sat, their backs against the chimneys, feeding the fire with the pages, and watching them burn yellow under the blue-black sky. Matteo fished the last piece from the sack. 'You've run out,' he said, and dropped it on the flames.

Instantly the fire around it turned green, and there was a sharp, acrid smell. Matteo jerked backwards, and Mercédès gasped – then darted her hand into the flames and snatched it back out.

'What *was* that?' she said, sucking at her palm. The paper was half-burned, and stained, but as they watched, words began to take shape on the blank paper: sharp black marks.

'Ink!' said Matteo.

The handwriting was old, and like none he'd ever seen. It was large and looped, beautiful: the writing of someone confident in their skill with a pen. The top part of the paper had burned away entirely, but it appeared to be some kind of letter.

'I've heard of this type of ink!' said Mercédès. She pressed her burned hand against the cold of the roof. 'They used it during the Revolution!'

Matteo read slowly, stumbling over some of the words:

'… and so I must congratulate you, reader, on discovering the secret of this paper! It is written with an invisible ink, from a recipe taught me, long ago, by a great man they called the Mad Priest. Most of my estate has been given to hospitals and schools, but I believe a city should have secrets, and diversions, and wonders. I have therefore added one of my own. I have left hidden in it a small part of my immense wealth: I have made this great city of Paris into a treasure hunt, with an X marks the spot. To solve it will take intelligence, and bravery, and hope, and luck. Your clue:

> 'There's silver vines amid the gold –
> Fruitfully search, for riches untold.
> Where the Sun King used to tread,
> Find the lid upon the nodding head.'

And under this, in a quicker hand:

> 'I cannot in fact call it untold riches, for riches have a 'way of getting told many times over. But it is valuable enough to transform a life.'

They stared at each other, and the air around them seemed to crackle.

'Treasure!' said Matteo. 'This must be what Danglars was looking for!'

'Riches untold!' said Mercédès.

'What's this, here?' Matteo pointed at the signature at the bottom of the paper. It was charred, but he could just read it. 'The Count of Monte … Cristo.'

'But that's the name!' cried Mercédès. 'That's the count,

Matteo! The Count of Monte Cristo! The man who used to live in this house! Oh, if only Clotilde had found out in time!'

'The treasure might not be real,' said Matteo. He tried very hard to sound sceptical, world-weary and tough-hearted – because inside, his heart was bounding so hard with hope it threatened to escape his chest. 'Or if it's real, it might not be there any more. Someone could have got there years ago.'

'How could they have, without the clue?' said Mercédès. 'No! We're going to find it, and get Clotilde and Églantine back into their apartment, Matteo! We are, aren't we?'

Matteo gave up on his sceptical face. He grinned. 'Who *doesn't* follow a treasure map?'

They pored over the paper. 'To start with,' said Mercédès, 'what's a Sun King?'

Matteo sorted through the piles in the back of his head. Some of them were rather dusty. 'Sol was the Roman god of the sun. Helios in Greek.'

Mercédès looked doubtful. 'What good are Greek and Roman gods? We're in France.' She stared down at the street below. It was empty, except for two women in fur muffs and fur-trimmed coats picking their way in high-buttoned boots over the dirt of the pavement. 'Maybe we could ask someone.'

'Who? Those women? *Excuse me, Madame, for hanging off the drainpipe while we talk, but do you know what is a Sun King?* They'd think we were pickpockets and call the police.'

'Fine.' Mercédès stole one more look at the women: one of them had paused to adjust the ostrich feathers in her hat; the wind was growing fierce, and the feathers were threatening to take flight. 'We'll work it out ourselves!'

She had spoken more loudly than she'd intended, and the woman in the hat looked up, squinting through the evening towards them.

'Get down!'

They ducked low, and the black kittens took the opportunity to leap upon Matteo's face and claw joyfully at his eyebrows. He reached up to protect his eyes, and the ginger cat pounced on the paper.

'Give that back!' Matteo snatched at it, and missed.

One of the kittens, thrilled at the game, scrabbled at

the paper. The bottom half was still in the ginger's mouth as Mercédès seized hold of its hindquarters – the paper, caught in the kitten's claws, tore in two, and a gust of icy wind blew the top half off the roof.

'No!' Matteo lunged after it, both arms stretching out over the edge of the roof, but it was too late. The door below was opened just as the paper fluttered down on to the doorstep.

Far below, Danglars bent and picked it up. Very, very quietly, Matteo swore. Ignoring furious hisses from Mercédès, he leaned further over the edge, bending from the waist to better see the street below.

The man's whole attention was on the piece of paper in his hand. As Matteo watched, his mouth, illuminated by lamplight, stretched in a smile. From the wrinkles on his face, Matteo could tell that it was not a familiar happening. The skin stretched too tightly over his bones. He read it again, and fingered the torn edge.

'This is it! This is it!' He started to mutter under his breath; Matteo could only hear one word in two. 'But … the rest? Those women … hiding something … there must be more!' Danglars searched the ground, prodding it with his stick, but there were only leaves and pavement. At last he grunted, folded the paper, and put it in his top pocket. Round the side of the house was a white horse, and a groom: a short man with a smudged, ungenerous face. Danglars dismissed the groom, and mounted the horse.

Then he glanced up.

Matteo recoiled, jerking his head back from the edge, pressing himself down and out of sight. He could feel his heart pounding against the roof: he thought it might burst out of his chest and lie beating on the slate. At last, there was the sound of hoofs moving away.

'Did he see you?' whispered Mercédès.

'I don't know. I don't think so. Maybe.' *Yes*, said the voice inside his chest. And the face that Matteo had looked into was not a kind one: pale, sharp-featured, the tilt to the brows of one accustomed to his own way. 'He's got the paper.'

'I saw.' Mercédès looked at the torn scrap in her hand. 'But he's only got the letter part,' she said. 'And the first two lines of the poem. He can't do much with that.'

'Maybe … maybe I stay here tonight,' said Matteo. 'Just in case of … you know. Just in case, just in case.' He did not think that the man would come swarming up the drainpipe. But it was a face that said it would be brutal if it wanted.

'Fine,' said Mercédès. Her voice was very low, and it quavered. 'You can sleep under the Persians.'

Few people have the chance to sleep under a pile of eight Persian cats. The claws get in your thighs and arms, but their noses are very soft against your cheek, and a tail draped around your neck makes the softest scarf. The purring makes a very fine lullaby.

The purring was loud enough, indeed, to drown out the noise of footsteps returning, just before dawn, and a man's boots pacing below, as he waited for the children to come down.

CHAPTER FIVE

M atteo woke early, with a face full of cat. A grocer pushed an apple cart down the street, bellowing his refrain. 'Apples! Ripe apples, fine apples, discount apples for the pot!'

The apples, and his dreams, and the fact he was accidentally wearing the cat's bottom as a blindfold, all mixed together in his head. It took Matteo a moment to work out where he was – and then all the memories of the day before came sweeping back, and he sat bolt upright. There was fear, cold and hard in his stomach; but there was a buzzing in his blood too.

Hidden treasure! he thought. *Gold, perhaps. Gold!* He had never been the kind of boy who expects to have anything to do with treasure. He thought of striding into the bakery and buying one of everything in it – eclairs with vanilla cream, brioches filled with chocolate custard, enormous strawberry tarts and soft yellow madeleine cakes topped with candied cherries. And then he thought of Églantine, her gnarled hand clutching at her violin, and Clotilde, her hair dipping in the mud-and-horse-manure mixture that coats the Paris streets after rain, and his whole body shook with the thought.

The apple-seller sent up his cry again. Matteo's stomach growled. It was very early, and the light was the grey thin of the dawn. The apples looked very red, and his mouth still tasted of the burned pigeon he had eaten at lunch. He could be down the drainpipe in less than a minute, and up it in less than two. He scratched a message in the ashes for Mercédès, who was still asleep under a carpet of breathing fur: *gon for brekfast*.

He spat on his palms, and shinned down the drainpipe. The thought of eating something that was not slightly burned gave him even greater speed than usual, and it took him forty-seven seconds to get from leaning against the chimney pots to standing on the ground.

It took him ten seconds to cross the road, keeping his head down and wearing his most invisible face – a little sullen, chin down, hands in pockets. He did not see the figure down the road jerk into alertness and follow him.

The apple-seller was leaning against a lamp post, talking to a labourer with a wide grin and a harelip. Matteo leaned casually against the cart, pretending to tie his bootlace. As he straightened up he grabbed two apples in each fist, and was halfway over the road again when a hand closed on his shoulder.

The apple-seller, he thought, and swore under his breath, turning – to see Danglars, his suit rumpled, his face wet with sweat. His fury was so vicious Matteo could smell it – it was in his sweat, hot and rotting.

'You! Don't try to run – I saw you up there! I've been waiting for you!'

He was white, and his lips were purplish. His eyebrows were so light they were almost invisible, and made his face look featureless – like a wet sheet pressed against a skull.

'Where's the rest of that paper? Did you burn it? It's mine, by rights!' Spit flew from his mouth as he spoke.

'Get off me!' Matteo twisted, and the man's grip went deeper into his arm, the nails against his skin.

'My grandfather was ruined by the Count of Monte Cristo – disgraced! Driven out of Paris! Cristo's wealth should have been *my* wealth. The treasure is mine!'

'I don't know anything about any paper!' said Matteo.

'Liar!' spat Danglars, which was true.

'I'm not!' said Matteo, which was not – but which was, he felt, justified in the circumstances.

Danglars' voice was tight and clipped, but his eyes were wild. 'I knew that part of Monte Cristo's fortune was still out there – I knew he had hidden it! I searched and searched for any trace of it! They said I was mad, but I was *right*. What is the rest of the clue? Tell me!'

Matteo did not think it was the right time for an in-depth conversation. He kicked, as hard as he could, at the man's shins, and ran. Matteo knew about shins. There are, of course, other places that you can kick, but shins give the best return for your efforts.

He did not think Danglars would chase him – not properly, not in broad daylight. He was wrong. He turned at the corner and saw him pushing aside a man selling shoe polish from a tray, scattering the man's little pots. Matteo scanned the buildings as he flashed past, but none were right – the drainpipes looked like they would need careful handling, and he had no time for that.

A great shout came from behind him, and a cry – 'Stop him!' – and Matteo dodged a stern old woman with a stick, and ran on. It was market day, and that helped. Farmers were herding sheep and cows into the centre of the city, and tending to geese in horse-drawn carts. He gave a pull at the back of a cart as he passed, and three pigs came hurtling after him. *The more chaos the better*, he thought. Sometimes, a little chaos is exactly what you need.

The Jardins des Champs-Élysées came in sight, and he swerved towards them. A tree! That was what he needed.

The gardens were large, with a pavilion to the north and a fountain to the south – and achingly fashionable. This was where people came to test the effect of their newest and more enormous hats, and to exercise small dogs, some of whom, when it rained, wore hats bigger than their owners'. Matteo did not admire the dogs, and had plans to steal the hats for himself, one day. But now it was not yet 6 a.m., and it was deserted. Matteo vaulted over the fence and hurled himself down the avenue, gravel flying behind him, flanked either side by trees as high as churches.

He leaped into the branches, feeling the reassuring bite of the bark against his palms. He stilled its shaking leaves just four seconds before Danglars appeared. His hair was slick with sweat and his face was grey with rage.

'I know you're here. Come down, and we'll talk. I just want to know what you know! I can give you money.'

Silence. There was rustling in a tree further down the avenue. Danglars stiffened and walked right past him.

The coaxing had gone from his voice. He sighed. 'Every second you stay hidden makes it worse for you when I do find you.'

A tree rustled again, but a different one this time, opposite Matteo.

'If you're not going to help me, you will have made an enemy. Do you understand? Don't expect me to have pity. You *don't matter*. I could throw you in the river and never once think of you again, boy. A child with no parents, no friends: a child all alone! Whom nobody cares about! It would be as easy as snuffing out the light of a very small candle.'

Matteo stared down at the man: at his curving mouth, his pinched nostrils. Matteo neither nodded nor shook his head; he only watched.

'People don't care about most things, you know, once you teach them how not to. They're just *longing* for permission not to care. The craving – my God, the craving to be allowed not to care! It could eat the whole world.'

Matteo reached up to the branch ahead of him and pulled himself higher. The branches shifted under him, and Danglars' head turned.

As it turned, an apple, grey with mould on one side, hit Danglars full in the eye.

He froze, and the muscles in his neck grew so tight they stood out, ridges in a rock.

There was a silence, of exactly three seconds. And then the air was suddenly filled with flying things: apples riddled with wasps, old conkers, a policeman's shoe, stones, branches, a hat that had once belonged to a dog – hailing from every tree on either side of the avenue. Danglars might have been able to withstand it – he was as ruthless with himself as he was with others – but then a sudden cascade of sunflower seeds was thrown over his head. It pooled in every part of his suit, and as it fell over him the birds came at him. Crows and seagulls, one surprisingly ravenous robin, and dozens and dozens of pigeons, pecking and stabbing, their claws catching in his collar.

Danglars ducked, protecting his eyes with his arm. 'Stay out of it, boy! You have no idea what you're doing.' And he tore the paper from his pocket, batting away at the wings in his face. 'I'll be watching you. Everywhere you go, I'll know! I'll haunt you, and I'll destroy you.' He twisted, calling up at the trees around him. 'You're not safe, boy! You'll never be safe again.'

And he half ran, half strode away down and out of the park.

Matteo was left in the tree: his whole body thrumming with raw, bright shock.

There was an owl hoot and a single shout of glee, and suddenly the entire avenue of trees was shaking, as if the trees themselves were laughing.

A girl who looked barely seven years old appeared in the leaves above him, pale-skinned, with her hair trailing behind her for a full metre and tangling in the branches; and then another girl, older than him, dark-skinned, with a hiccuping laugh and shoes made from oak leaves – and a third, and a fourth. Within a minute and a half there were thirteen girls lounging in the branches around him, or swinging by a crooked elbow – or, in the case of the smallest, hanging upside down by a single ankle and plaiting her hair.

They were all whispering among themselves as they came, but not in a language he knew. They eyed him with the detached interest you might give to a farm animal.

'I ...' Matteo had never been so entirely lost for words. He had never seen children who radiated such pure wildness. 'I ... I should thank you,' he said. 'That was you, wasn't it?'

A redhead with a sharpened flint in her belt held up her hand.

'No thanksings. We don't have no use for them. Just because we got rid-chucked of him, doesn't mean we won't kick-off you too.'

Matteo found his heart was still beating double time. 'What?'

'Do you not speak plain French?' said another, a girl with huge dark eyes, and she turned upside down, hanging casually by her knees. 'We said, just because we helped you, doesn't mean we're friendship-hunting.'

Matteo was rather stung. 'Why did you help me, then?'

'We didn't want him coming ups and inspecting the trees, no?'

'Where … What … ?' He realised it wasn't going to come out right. His sentences often didn't. He rarely let it bother him – after all, he spoke to very few people, and he liked it that way – but it was important, now, to get it right. 'Do you live here?'

'Yup!' said the smallest girl. 'All year long, rain or shine. Tree-dwellers, aren't we? Sky-dancers. You're trespassing on our abode. Off you tiddle, I'd say.'

'Ha! Look at his face! All sullened-up and anger-patched.'

Matteo could feel himself blushing. It was true he had scowled – but he had every right, he thought, to scowl.

One of the girls broke out into another language.

'She says, you're not what we were wanting today,' said another.

'No she didn't,' said Matteo.

'In Italian she did.'

'We all,' said another girl, one with straight black eye-brows, a great cloud of black curls and sardonic eyes, 'speak two or three languages. English, German, Italian …'

'Arabic, Turkish, Ndebele, Shona.'

'Some of us seven.'

'Me nine, I think.'

'How?'

'We listen to the tourists, in the summers, down below. We collect their words.'

'Though we're not always so magnificently sure which words belong to which.'

'And some words are uglificators, so we turn out new ones.'

A brunette stood up and walked her branch like a tightrope. 'We can,' she said, suddenly smart-voiced, 'of course speak the most exquisite French, should we wish it.' She spoke as though she were about to cut the ribbon on a new hospital. 'The President – Émile, we call him Émi – likes to walk with his spaniel below us. We know more about economic policy and the senate than almost anyone else in France, us tree-dwellers.'

'Are there more of you?'

'Tree-dwellers? Of course. There are girls down by the Jardin des Plantes: Safi and Anastasia. They keep to themselves, private-quiet-like, but Safi can climb faster than anyone in Paris. We're everywhere.'

Matteo felt his head turn giddy at the thought of it: and

he found himself glowering at his past self. All this time! He, a Parisian to his fingertips, had never suspected the existence of such children. Why had he never properly looked up? What other secrets lay only just hidden above the surface of the city? Roughly he pushed back the leaves and looked out, and for the first time he felt the air vibrate with all the human dreams and strangenesses, just out of sight.

'He's glaring at the air now,' said one of the girls. 'Getting cross at the wind.'

He turned back to the girls. He had questions. 'How do you not fall out of the trees when you sleep?'

'We tie ourselves in. Sleep-knots.'

'We make pillows from the ladies' fur muffs.'

'We take them when they forget them on the benches ...'

'We take them, to be honest, even when they *don't* forget them on the benches.'

'And we tie the muffs to the branches. We sleep well, up here. And we keep conkers in our pockets at night, just in case.'

There was something a little alarming about them. Matteo was not in the habit of being afraid of other children – his reckoning was, he was faster than most if it came to a chase, and so there was no point – but if he *was* going to be afraid, it would be of these ones.

'Now!' said the oldest. 'Girls, are we agreed? Out?'

'Agreed!'

'We would like you to offity-shove.' She clapped her hands, and immediately the girls began to talk all at once, and to throw bits of branches and leaves at him.

'*Geh weg!*'

'*Zou kai!*'

'We have had sufficient portions of your particular recipe of uninteresting.'

'We require the oxygen you are snorting.'

'No offence meant. Or at least, not much. A middle-helping, size-medium, neither-here-nor-there amount, yes?'

'Don't come back, or we'll stick-and-conker you.'

'We'll unlace your intestines and use them for skipping ropes.'

'Vanquishments, that's what we like!'

'Wait – wait a second!' said Matteo.

'No. We've reached the end of you.' One of the girls bared her teeth and flicked her hair.

'I just want to know – do you know who the Sun King is?'

The girls looked at each other, from girl to girl. Heads shook. Then the tallest said, 'Xavier would know.'

'Who's Xavier?' said Matteo.

'How do you not know about Xavier? Xavier knows more about Paris than any person, street-bound or skystepper.'

'Right. But, listen – Stop throwing things for just a second! How can I get to him?'

'He's the eyes of Paris. He keeps the central watch. So. He's in the centre.'

Matteo could feel his temper slipping away from him: a stone rolling downhill. 'That doesn't actually help,' he said.

'Xavier's triumphant!' said one of the girls, and snorted.

'Now go.' One of the smallest girls reached into her pocket and brought out a conker the size of her own fist. She tossed it, threatening, into the air. 'You don't want us to ammunition you. I promise, you don't.'

Matteo glanced around. At the far end of the avenue there was a church. Its drainpipe looked respectable. He could get up there and make a plan in the safety of the roof tiles. He swung down from the trees, and was just about to make a sprint for it when the oldest girl's voice rang out again.

'One thing!'

She stuck her head out from the very top of the tree, six metres up in the sky.

'If you go to see Xavier, you need to take payment. He doesn't help anyone without a gift. He's not nice – not like us.'

'What kind of gift?'

She laughed. 'What are the things you yourself want most, boyo? Whatever it is, is the thing you should give!'

Safely up on the church rooftop, leaning against the base of the spire, Matteo allowed himself to concentrate. *The centre*, they'd said – but nobody agreed where the exact centre of the city was. Most people said it was Notre-Dame, but some people said it was the new Eiffel Tower. But … *triumphant*?

And then Matteo knew: the Arc de Triomphe, the great stone arch built for Napoleon's triumphant parade through the city, was on a vast roundabout at the heart of the city, at the centre of a star-shape of twelve streets fanning outwards.

Matteo could feel his palms becoming hot. The Arc was fifty metres high, dwarfing the great halls and stores around it: more than thirty times his own height. If he fell, he would fall thirty of himself. It was not a nice thought.

Well, he told himself. *I'll just have to not fall, I suppose.*

CHAPTER SIX

The thing Matteo wanted most was food. He wished he hadn't dropped the apples: he could have given them to Xavier. But there were other foods to be had, if you didn't mind a certain amount of lawbreaking.

He discussed it with Mercédès, back up on the rooftop. He told her everything: of Danglars and his threats, and the girls. He had expected her to be as astonished as he had been at the news of the children in the trees, but she wasn't.

She nodded. 'I see shadows. They could be cats, or mirages – you blink and they're gone. But I always thought … *maybe*. It helped, sometimes, at night, when I was alone.'

Mostly, though, they had discussed the problem of food. 'It'll have to be luxurious,' she said. 'You couldn't just bring someone half a blackbird and expect them to tell you their secrets. What's your favourite food?'

'Steak. With fresh bread and butter.'

'Good. Mine too.'

The stealing of the steak and butter was easy, or easy enough. The carrying it was harder – the meat, cut into half a dozen thick slices, wouldn't fit in his pockets, so he wrapped it in newspaper, and added an onion and a hunk of bread he borrowed from a child while its back was turned, and tied it across his shoulders.

They waited until the real dark – the deep, settled dark that came between two and three in the morning, when only the most determined drinkers were still in the bars – to set out. Matteo glanced over his shoulder so many times his neck grew stiff and aching with it. The beat of his blood said, *Danglars … Danglars … Danglars.*

They went as far as they could by rooftop until, at the last, they had to go on the ground. Mercédès slid down the drainpipe of an oyster restaurant, slowly, her feet scrabbling against the wall, her face grim. Matteo followed, hand over hand – it was starting to feel natural, like walking downstairs.

They darted over an entirely empty, pitch-black road, to

where the Arc de Triomphe, in the centre of the great ring of roads, stood watch over the city.

Mercédès looked up at its towering height, and put out a hand to steady herself on Matteo's shoulder.

'No,' she breathed. 'Absolutely not.'

'No what?'

'I can't climb it,' said Mercédès. 'I thought maybe I could, but I can't.'

'Of course you can.' But he was aware that he did not sound convincing. It did not, looming up towards the stars above them, look one hundred per cent undeadly.

'No. If I tried, I would panic, and slip, and die.'

'Fine,' said Matteo. 'I'll go. You wait here, and if anyone comes in sight, you call – do a scream like a cat – and I'll …'

'Do what, exactly? Where are you going to hide, mid-wall?'

'I'll stop moving. It's dark: they might not see me if I freeze.'

There was no drainpipe: only great slabs of brick, with deep grooves in between. He gave his boots to Mercédès, set his toes in the first gap, and took hold of the wall.

'Wait!' said Mercédès.

'What?'

'Do you think I'm a coward? Because I'm not, you know. It's not cowardice: it's just plain sense, if I know I'd die doing it.'

Matteo looked at her – at the blisters on her fingers from practising with her rapier, at the scratches from the cats – and grinned. 'I don't think you're a coward. And you shouldn't care even if I did.'

He began to wonder, soon, if it wouldn't have been much more pleasant to forget the treasure and stay on the ground. He pulled, and reached, and pulled again. He found his hands were shaking. He paused, waiting for the blood in his fingers to calm, but when that did not work, he had no choice but to continue with shaking hands.

You must never, when climbing, look down. Usually that was easy, Matteo thought; you looked up instead. But when climbing something fifty metres high, it is best neither up nor down – only at the place your hands were right at that moment, and at the place they would be in the next five seconds. Anything more, and your hands surrender to the vertigo-whisper that says, What if you let go? and you fall thirty of yourself to the ground.

His arms were close to finished when he finally came in sight of the top. Matteo seized the edge of the roof like it was a life jacket in a storm, and swung himself up over the top. Every single muscle in his body was shaking. For a moment, he could see nothing but a blur.

The blur spoke. 'It's always frightening the first time you do it. Did you panic?'

Matteo considered whether to be honest. 'Once. My hands went weird.'

'Good answer! Here's a fact for free: if you can feel yourself panicking, it's a sign you're not yet one hundred per cent scared. Once you are as mad-scared as it is humanly possible for you to be, you'll be as calm as the River Seine in the sun.'

And then there was a laugh, and the blur became a boy, standing in the middle of the great arch, hands on hips, waiting.

'You're from on top of the Opera House, no? And then the old Monte Cristo house.'

The boy was as tall as a man; he might, Matteo thought, have been seventeen. He had crooked teeth, which showed in a sardonic smile.

Matteo swallowed and straightened up. 'How did you know? Can you see it from here?'

'I can see the Cristo house from here. There – you can't miss it – it's the tallest in the whole arrondissement. And besides, I get messages. Via pigeons, crows, seagulls. Sometimes robins, although they're not very bright – it's hard to make them understand where to go.'

'From who? Those girls in the trees?'

The boy looked hard at Matteo. 'I tell nothing for nothing. Before we start – what did you bring?'

The parcel felt reassuringly large as he handed it over. Xavier did not say anything as he opened it, so Matteo didn't either. Instead he watched as the older boy went to the very centre of the top of the Arc, where there lay a pile of wood which he set alight. He produced a real cast-iron frying pan. He added three slices of meat, looked again at Matteo from head to toe, and added two more, leaving two in the package.

Then he sat down, cross-legged, and pointed at the spot opposite him. 'Sit.'

Matteo sat, and smiled a half-smile. He usually resented being told what to do – but when a boy who lives astride the tallest arch in the world tells you to sit, you do.

'Right. What do you want? Want to know who's planning to rig the next local election in Aix-en-Provence? I can tell you that. Want to know why there's about to be a terrible scandal when it comes out what the War Minister's been doing? I can tell you, but I'd need more beef.'

'No,' said Matteo. 'But how do *you* know those things?'

'I hear snippets on the wind. I see things through windows. I put things together. People tell me things – politicians, countesses – in exchange for news about other things. I leave a string hanging down to the pavement, from one to two a.m., Tuesdays and Thursdays. People tie notes with news for me, and I send notes down in return.'

Matteo waited, while the boy poked at the steak. And then: 'I need to know … Who or what is a Sun King?'

The boy snorted. 'Is that all?' Matteo couldn't tell if it was sarcasm or not.

'And I want to know whatever you know about a man called Danglars.'

Xavier rocked back on his haunches. 'Danglars. He's …' And Xavier swore, a word that made a passing pigeon blink in shock. 'He's … I would say, a little deranged. He thinks about nothing but money. Literally, nothing nothing nothing. You think those people don't exist? That everyone cares about something else – their mother, or their dog, or their work? No. He cares only about money, and the power it will give him. He's not starving, or anything like that – but he's not the richest man in Paris, and he thinks he deserves to be. He's the grandson of a famous banker. The family lost all their money, and there was a huge disgrace.'

'Yes,' said Matteo. 'He said so – or rather, he spat it at me. He said it was the fault of the Count of Monte Cristo.'

Xavier snorted. 'When the Count of Monte Cristo was young, three men betrayed him: he was sent to prison for a crime he didn't commit, but he escaped, and became wildly wealthy. And then he spent years taking revenge on the men: one of the men shot himself, one went mad – it was very dramatic. And the third of them, a very powerful banker, was publicly disgraced, caught stealing money. He was Danglars' grandfather. And Danglars has become obsessed – *obsessed* – with clawing his way back to what his grandfather had been. For the last year, I've seen him everywhere in Paris – searching, searching, for the Count's treasure. He's vowed, when he finds it, to destroy every building named after the Count, every hospital, every school: all of it.'

Matteo sat up straighter. 'So it's real? The treasure?'

Xavier shrugged. 'Maybe. The Count gave almost all of his money away before he died. He was not a good man – he did both great and terrible things – but he didn't want to die rich. And, as he was dying, he still had a box full of jewels – diamonds, rubies as big as your eye, sapphires like marbles, strings of pearls as long as a skipping rope – and so, the story goes, he hid them. Nobody knows where. They say there are clues across the whole of Paris.'

The boy yawned and stretched. 'But that could be a myth. It was before your parents were born. There's almost nothing that we know for sure is true – just that he lived, briefly, in the Monte Cristo house – between the Champs-Élysées and the Rue de Ponthieu. And a few months ago, Danglars had the idea that the treasure might be in the house. I heard he found a way to kick the old women out, so he could search it – is that true?'

Matteo nodded. 'He threw them out into the street.'

Xavier cracked his knuckles. 'He wouldn't care about old women – I don't think he really believes they're real living people. I'm not sure he really believes anyone is quite real, except himself.'

This did not sound likely to Matteo. 'What does he think we are then – rubber dolls?'

'No.' The boy rose and walked to the edge. 'I mean … You know the way, if you try to find the very end of your thoughts, you never can?' He set both hands on the stone, his fingers curling over the edge, and kicked up into a handstand. 'If you try to imagine the heart of yourself, it's somewhere hot and deep and strange and buried? I don't think he believes other people are like that. I think he thinks they're just … blank inside.' He straightened up. 'You understand? Blank, and dull, like sand. It's the stupidest thing you can do – to refuse to imagine other people are as endless as you are.' And he spat over the edge.

Matteo imagined the spit travelling hundreds of feet: it made his insides shake, and he poked at the pan. 'Hey!' said Xavier, and Matteo jumped. 'Keep your hands out of my meat.'

They sat side by side, eating steak sandwiches – Xavier gave Matteo only one piece: 'It was a present,' he said, 'and I'm eating it myself.' Their legs dangled over the edge, Matteo's feet cold in the night air.

'What was the other thing?'

'The Sun King.' Matteo explained about the letter, and the astonishment of the appearing ink. Xavier's eyes had the look of someone filing it away, for later.

'Tell me the clue – the exact words?'

Matteo recited it from memory: it was not the kind of thing he felt at any risk of forgetting:

'There's silver vines amid the gold –
Fruitfully search, for riches untold.
Where the Sun King used to tread,
Find the lid upon the nodding head.'

Xavier took hold of his ankle, pulled it round behind his neck, and held it, stretching the muscle. 'You really don't know who the Sun King is? What do they teach you at school these days?'

'I wouldn't know,' said Matteo. 'I've never really been to one.'

Xavier repeated the procedure with the other leg. 'The Sun King is King Louis the Fourteenth of France! He became king at the age of four, which must have been very confusing for him, and then he married his cousin and ruled for seventy-two years. He died about two hundred years ago. But most of all – he built the Palace of Versailles. You *must* have heard of Versailles?'

Matteo nodded. Everyone in France has heard of Versailles – the greatest, largest and most gold-edged palace in the world. 'Of course I've heard of it – but I have no idea how to get there. It's out in the countryside, isn't it?'

Xavier nodded. 'I can draw you a map.' He opened a coffee tin and took from it a scrap of paper and a pen. 'Look – here's a map of Paris.' And he drew fast, labelling as he went: 'There's your Opera House … there's the old Monte Cristo house. Here's the Eiffel Tower … here's the Louvre, Notre-Dame, here's the church of Sacré-Coeur. Here's me. And *this* –' he drew a line and an arrow – 'is the road out to Versailles. It's straight all the way – about four or five hours' walk.'

Matteo's heart sank. 'Five hours?' Even if they went at first light, that was slow. 'The thing is, if Danglars is watching us, that's a long time on the open road.'

Xavier stretched both legs in front of him and rested his forehead on them. His voice, when he spoke, was muffled by his knees. 'You go via the ice cart: it comes from Le Havre to Paris, then on to the castle at Dreux, so that they can have sorbet at dinner, and down to Chartres, so the pilgrims to the cathedral there can have ice cream – but Versailles is right on the road to Dreux. The cart goes from the church of Sacré-Coeur every morning at six a.m. You climb in under the sacking.'

'On top of the blocks of ice?'

'Exactly. Just don't let them see you. They're not friendly if they catch you.'

'You want me to hide in an ice cart? Isn't that … quite cold?'

'I don't *want* you to do anything. You're welcome to take a private four-horse carriage, if you happen to be much richer than you look.'

'And when I get there, how do I get in?'

'You won't need to break in. Just go via the top.'

'You mean – the roof?'

'Yes,' he said, 'obviously! But – listen – you'll meet Leo and Anton. The Vampa boys. Be careful of Anton.'

'What do you mean?'

'Do you have any more meat?'

'No.'

'Then that's all I'm telling you.' Xavier dropped the last of his sandwich over the edge and lay back as it fell, staring up at the sky. 'So … you're one of us now?' said Xavier.

'Us?'

'You know. Skysteppers. There are a lot more of us than you'd think, across the city. Maybe in every city in the world, I don't know. Did you think it was just me and that girl on the Cristo house, and the tree-dwellers?'

'No,' said Matteo, and glared at his toes.

'If you have a good idea,' said Xavier, 'mostly, some other person will have had it too.'

'How many?'

Xavier shrugged and kicked his heels against the stonework. 'It's always changing. Tree-dwellers, church-hoppers, rooftoppers. We're all part of the same. Some of us aren't nice at all. There are the *gariers*, by the station – I'd stay away from them, if you enjoy having all your fingers attached to your hands. But we all belong up here.'

Matteo took the last bite of his sandwich. The height made it taste better: sweeter, and fatter. 'I didn't know,' he said. A new and peculiar feeling was rising in him, a spark reaching all the way from his stomach to his nose. There was a name, then, for what he was. A skystepper. A rooftopper.

There was the sudden scream of a cat, and both boys pressed themselves flat on the stone. Xavier's breathing was entirely unchanged, and Matteo tried to arrange his face to look as unconcerned as the older boy's. It was in the eyebrows, he thought, and with his fingers he made sure that his rested on the spot that means 'nonchalant'.

He did not feel nonchalant.

He counted to five, then swivelled on to his stomach and stared over the edge, seeking Mercédès.

Mercédès was almost invisible, pressed back against the shadows. But striding down the centre of the road away from them was a figure in a flapping coat, and above it an unusually white face.

'Danglars?' breathed Matteo.

'Maybe. On the prowl. Did anyone see you come this way? Anyone in any of the bars?'

'I don't know! Maybe.'

Xavier stuck his finger in the frying pan and licked the grease. 'You should go. But you need to be careful around him. He's full of fear and chaos and rage. He has a stomach full of *no*: *no* bubbling in his bloodstream and little microscopic *no*es lying on his tongue. Those people aren't safe to be around.'

CHAPTER SEVEN

The ice cart left at 6 a.m., which meant it was 5 a.m. when Matteo approached the trees of the treedwellers. They did not take kindly to being woken. It took some time for the shower of sticks thrown at his head to die down.

At last he said: 'Can you do something? A favour? I could owe you one in exchange?'

The tallest and most alarmingly beautiful of the girls did a handstand on the branch. She spoke with her hair in her eyes.

'Favours aren't something we enjoy. You tell us what it is. If it sounds our kind of excitement, yes. If it sounds boring like a schoolroom, no.'

The others clustered round, their eyes curious. 'Audra's right.'

A dark-haired, round-faced girl nudged him nearly off his branch. 'Spill, roof boy.'

'There are two old women,' said Matteo, 'somewhere in the city. I don't know where they've gone. They're easy to recognise – one has hair down to the floor, and one's so tall she practically touches the door frame …' and he described, as best he could, the two women's clothes and shoes and eyes. 'Can you find them?'

'And if we can?' said the little redhead. 'You want them stick-and-conkered? Like we did with the white-faced man?'

'What? No! I want them looked after. I want to know they're OK.'

'Why do you care?'

Briefly Matteo told them what had happened. 'It was …' He did not want to say how bitterly it had hurt him to see an old woman weep; and how much it had felt like something he had seen before. 'I didn't mean to care, but … now I can't un-care. I tried – but it's not reversible.'

The redhead nodded, as if this were something she understood. She picked her nose and wiped it on a passing squirrel. 'We'll see to it.'

Matteo nodded his thanks. 'I was just thinking, you

know … it's going to get cold soon. The outdoors is no place for old women.'

And the tree full of girls, barefoot and rag-clad, nodded solemnly in agreement.

The journey to Versailles was not a comfortable one. They hid behind a large group of nuns outside the great church of Sacré-Coeur, and darted into the ice cart just as it set off out of the city. One of the nuns saw them, but she only raised her eyebrows and winked.

The blocks of ice, each as large as a pillar box, were wrapped in brown sacking, and they discovered that the only way to fit was to lie on their backs on top of them, hidden under the canvas roof.

'Stop wriggling,' hissed Mercédès.

'I don't *wriggle*. I'm reorganising my legs, it's different.'

It was not only the nun who saw them go. A short man with a smudged, ungenerous face blinked, in half-remembered recognition. The children, intent on scrabbling over the ice, did not see. The man frowned, then mounted his brown cob, and followed.

Within half an hour, Matteo's legs were so cold they felt like they might belong to someone else. By the time they were nearing Versailles and it was time to slip out and jump down on to the dusty road, his skin had turned blue, to match the morning sky.

'I think,' he said, as they walked up the long drive, 'I might have refrigerated myself beyond the point of return.' The drive was so overgrown with weeds and bushes that it looked like something out of a fairytale: one of the darker ones, he thought, where princes get eaten.

'I think my knees are about to drop off,' said Mercédès. 'Have you ever heard of that happening?'

But then they came in sight of the palace, and stopped talking.

The first thing any visitor to Versailles notices is that it is too large for one king, really, even if that king was unusually large. Built across multiple courtyards, jutting out into great sweeps of annexes and east and west wings, it has two thousand windows and more than a thousand chimneys. It was as though the King had ordered his architects to keep building, and had forgotten to say *stop*.

The second thing Matteo saw, as he came closer, was that it shone. It was limestone, but it was so rich a yellow he would not have been surprised if he had rubbed his hand along its walls and come away stained in gold. It was very obviously abandoned, and some of the windows were cracked, and roses grew up the side of one wall, which in the time of the kings would never have been allowed – but it was an astonishing thing.

Matteo had never seen anything so vast. He had seen large buildings – indeed, he had sat on top of many, for Paris likes its buildings imposing and its boulevards wide. He had not seen anything like this.

'It's … like a city. Like a city crammed into one building.'

'Come on. Let's get it over with.' Mercédès' lips had turned green at the edges. 'Let's climb it.'

Looking back, Matteo would have found it hard to describe the climb: it was made complicated by the fact that Mercédès insisted on doing it with one eye closed and then the other, alternately.

'I can't look with both at once. It'll be too much, and I'll die of it.'

He climbed a few metres below her, so as to catch her (although, he thought, if she *did* fall, he'd be unlikely to do anything other than fall with her). But, astonishingly, there was a triumphant shout, and Mercédès grasped the top of the carved parapet, and they were up, gulping in the clear morning air.

74

The roof stretched as far as half a dozen tennis courts in both directions. At the far end, crouched over something, his head bent in concentration, was a boy. He was very small – Matteo was bad at guessing ages, but perhaps seven, perhaps eight. He looked up, jumped to his feet, and came running at them.

'Uh-oh,' breathed Mercédès. Matteo was just debating the ethics of jabbing somebody so much smaller than him in the eye with a stick, when the boy reached them. He beamed. It was a peculiar face, Matteo thought – it seemed to have more ear and mouth than most people's, and his smile gave the impression of taking up at least three to four metres.

'You're here!'

Matteo had never, in his entire life, been greeted with such enthusiasm. 'Were you expecting us?'

'No! But you're here!' The boy, up close, was astonishing to look at. He was very thin and his skin was pale, but so freckly he looked almost tanned. His fingers were very long, and his hands looked older than the rest of him. But what was startling was his clothes: his trousers were made up, patchwork, of a dozen pieces of different green silks, and his jacket was the same, only in different pieces of embroidered blue velvet. 'You came all the way up the wall to see us – that's got to be worth something!'

'Oh. Well – I'm Mercédès,' said Mercédès, 'and this is Matteo. And we need your help.'

The boy nodded. 'I'm Leo. Leo Vampa.' He turned to Matteo. 'I don't like your trousers.'

Matteo had never had his clothing commented on. It was a novel experience, and not one he enjoyed. 'I didn't choose them. I found them, last year. And I don't care if you don't like them.'

'Are the trousers … important?' said Mercédès.

'Yes. I can help you, but not if he's going to be wearing those trousers. Brown is not a colour.'

He led them back across the slate, to where he had been sitting.

'You know, Louis the Fourteenth cared so much about clothes, he made it illegal to go into his gardens if you weren't dressed properly. Not everyone could afford the right clothes, so there were shops where you could rent silk dresses and jackets, just to be able to go in and smell the roses. But all those shops are gone now, and it's just us. Just me, and Anton, and my work. See!'

Laid out in the sun were hundreds and hundreds of

strips of cloth: most of them silk or satin or velvet, embroidered in gold and silver threads. Hanging on a rail built from the branches of an oak tree, there were clothes: trousers, shorts, jackets, dresses that would sweep the floor, and skirts that would stick out like a tutu in ravishing blues and silvers.

'I make them. But I don't have anyone to give them to. Not many people visit us, and they're making the palace into a museum, but for now it's just the caretaker, and he doesn't look the sort who would enjoy brocaded silk.'

'Where do you get the cloth?' asked Mercédès. She touched the edge of a deep rose-pink dress, and a little gasp of air came from her as if against her will.

'There are more than seven hundred rooms in the palace. I go in most nights. I cut the bottom inch off the curtains. I sew it up again. I come back. Most rooms have four windows at least, and each window has two curtains. Which means – I worked it out once – fourteen thousand, two hundred centimetres of material: I could dress a man who was half the height of the Eiffel Tower. Here: for you.' And he handed Matteo a pair of red trousers, stitched with gold, from the pile. 'Put these on, and then I can listen to you without wincing.'

They fitted well, if he turned up the bottoms. Matteo tucked his shirt into them, and stood, self-conscious, while Leo circled him.

'You could explain why you're here,' said Leo, 'while I do adjustments.' And he sat down at Matteo's feet, took out an enormous pair of scissors, and began to snip and sew the hems.

Mercédès explained, as swiftly as she could, about Clotilde and Danglars and the treasure hunt. Leo was so excited he knocked over his jarful of pins.

'Treasure! Yes! I knew it! You had faces, when you came over the top, that said you were searching for something.' He got to his feet. 'There. I could take them in a little more at the waist, but I don't think it's necessary – and you're still growing.'

'Fine,' said Matteo. But he covered his approval with a blank expression. If the boy knew how much he liked them, he might try to make him pay, and he had no money.

There was a thump, and a voice behind them. 'Leo, you have to stop giving people clothes.' It was another boy – older, taller, with the same freckles, but very different eyes.

'I don't see why not,' said Leo. 'There's only so many

trousers one person can wear.' He turned to Matteo. 'This is Anton. He won't let me embroider his shirts. He likes them plain. It's very stupid.'

Anton's hair was bright white-blond, and his eyes were blue. His would have been the kind of face people use as a model when they want to paint an archangel, were it not for his nose. His nose looked like it was passing judgement on all it encountered.

'What's this?' He smiled, but it was not a smile like Leo's. It was an on-purpose, effort-and-gums smile. 'What's going on?'

'I'm Mercédès,' said Mercédès. 'And this is Matteo.'

'Who let you up here?'

'People don't *let* me do things,' said Matteo. 'I do them.'

Anton acted as if he had not spoken. 'But I don't think we expected visitors, did we, Leo?'

'They came to ask for help,' said Leo.

'Ah.' The smile flicked off like an electric light. 'I'm afraid helping isn't on our to-do list today.'

He came closer, and his eyes raked Matteo and Mercédès. He sniffed. Matteo had never seen such thin nostrils. 'Do feel free to leave as soon as you can. Or I'll have to kick you out, and that would be sad.'

'Don't listen to him,' said Leo. 'It's just, when you don't have doors and locks, you have to be a bit more abrupt.'

'We don't want to do any harm,' said Mercédès. 'We came because a clue told us to.'

'Well, you can leave because I told you to, can't you?' He bared his teeth at her. 'We don't want you. The more people up here, the more risk we get caught.'

'But I thought there was nobody here!' said Mercédès. She looked suddenly afraid, and stared around.

'There's been no kings living here, not since 1789,' said Leo. 'But there's a caretaker – it's his job to keep watch and take anyone he catches to the police, but mostly he drinks red wine and sings out of tune about the past. Anton, stop being an idiot. Of course we're going to help! They're searching for treasure!'

Anton blinked. 'What kind of treasure?'

'Hidden treasure!'

'Where?'

'Hidden in Paris.'

'Real? Do you mean it? Or story-book stuff?'

'Real,' said Mercédès. 'Honestly. Real, solid treasure.'

Instantly the smile flickered on again, red and wet. Matteo had no use for such a smile. He scowled instead.

'Well,' said Anton. 'What are we waiting for? As I said, helping is very much on our to-do list.'

'That's not what you said!' said Matteo.

'What do you mean? Yes it is.'

'But you just—'

'I assure you. You misheard. The wind, up here, it blows words out of shape.' And he laughed, and the smile widened and softened, and for a moment he looked genuinely friendly. 'What do you need to know?'

Mercédès, in a visible act of will, smiled back. 'We're following a clue.' And she told him, very swiftly, the story of the paper. She recited:

'There's silver vines amid the gold –
Fruitfully search, for riches untold.
Where the Sun King used to tread,
Find the lid upon the nodding head.'

Anton's eyes flicked back to wary. '*Lid upon the nodding head* – that makes no sense. Is this some kind of joke?'

'No!' said Mercédès. 'We were thinking it might be a crown. Is Louis the Fourteenth's crown here?'

'Of course not,' said Anton. 'Napoleon took them all, years ago.'

But Leo laughed in sudden delight. 'No! Not a crown! *Nodding* means sleeping! So we need his bedroom!'

Mercédès' eyes lit up. 'Can you take us there?' she said. 'We're in a hurry. The old women, you know ...'

Anton frowned. 'What have the old women got to do with it?'

'We need to get them back into their home,' said Mercédès, 'before they get ill. They're not strong and they're not safe – old people die outside in the cold!'

'*What?*' Anton's face was that of someone who, expecting to drink a glass of milk, finds it to be flour. 'You're not going to keep the treasure?'

'Did you not hear the bit,' said Matteo, 'when we told you two old women were out on the streets?'

'And the paper with the clue belonged to Clotilde's grandmama!' said Mercédès. 'The Count gave it to her! We wouldn't be here if it wasn't for her. And I'm her guard!'

Anton shook his head. 'You're insane. You're not their guard – you don't even know them!'

'I am *not* insane!' Mercédès twisted to face Anton, and her eyes were angry. 'You want to know why I do it? Fine! It's because I have nobody! Nobody cares about me! But I still get to care for other people, and nobody gets to embarrass me out of it – my caring belongs to *me*. I know I'm worth something, because I'm guarding something worth guarding. So there!'

Anton barked with amusement. Matteo was about to lunge at him, but Leo nodded once, quick and sharp and seeing. He walked straight to the stone balustrade that edged the roof, vaulted over it, landed, and crouched like a cat on the gold-painted window sill beneath. 'Too much talking! Just *come*!' he said, and slipped inside.

The light was dim inside the palace. The windows were so covered in grime it looked like evening, and as they walked through a vast mirrored hall as big as several football pitches, shadows hovered in every corner. The mirrors were so dusty Matteo could not see much more than a smudge for his reflection, and the floor was grey at the edges. But even so, it was a staggering thing. It was, he thought, designed to make you think, I *should probably do whatever the person who owns this room orders me*. It was a room designed to awe people into obedience.

'Smell that?' whispered Mercédès, up ahead, as they passed through a doorway and into a half-furnished drawing room, the furniture dim-gold. 'That's the scent of kings!'

'Do kings smell of damp?' said Matteo.

'You know what I mean.'

Anton followed behind them all on soundless feet. He kept a hand on the knife in his belt.

'This was a music room,' whispered Leo. 'See? The curtains are excellent in here: green, blue, purple – every colour. I made some summer shorts from these. Except there's no orange anywhere. The King went to war with William of Orange, and he said nobody could wear orange, and it stuck.'

'It's incredible.' Mercédès laid a hand on a grand piano, leaving a palm print behind in the dust. 'Look at this. Nobody's played it for so long.'

'And this,' said Leo, leading them into a vast room, the ceiling painted with gold, 'is where the Sun King ate. It was called the *Grand Couvert* – it was a great honour to come and watch him dine, and people used to bribe each other to get in. He'd have four bowls of different soups, and then a whole pheasant, and a partridge, a big plate of salad, maybe two slices of ham, and mutton with garlic, and a plate of pastries, fruit, and then hard-boiled eggs to finish.'

'Eggs?' said Mercédès. 'For dessert?'

'I know. It's not what I'd do if I was king, but there you are. And that, through there, is the state bedroom,' said Leo. 'If I was going to hide something, it's where I'd go – there's just so *much* of it. In here!'

The room was enormous, decked in gold and crimson. 'Your trousers come in part from these curtains,' said Leo to Matteo.

The walls were crowded with paintings of saints, and there was a wardrobe big enough to hide a horse in.

'For his jackets,' said Leo. 'And that one, over there, for his trousers. When he woke up, he had courtiers to dress him. He wasn't even allowed to put on his own *pants*. It was a great honour, to be chosen to put on the King's underwear.'

On the colossal marble fireplace there was a bust of a man with a sharp nose and a large curled wig.

'That's Louis the Fourteenth – the Sun King.'

'He had a statue ... of himself ... watching himself sleep?' said Matteo.

Leo nodded. 'They were very into that kind of thing. Kings loved a statue of themselves. I think they must have found it reassuring, or something. In case you start to doubt you actually exist. The French are very into that.'

'Right,' said Mercédès. 'The clue said his bed, so ... here it is.'

The bed was three times the usual size, with posts each side and a canopy stretched tight above in rich red velvet, embroidered in silver and gold.

'It's a bed – it's not a clue,' said Anton. 'This is absurd – it's just make-believe, isn't it? We need to go. Leo! Come on!'

'Shh,' said Leo.

Matteo walked around the bed, staring at it from every angle. He lifted the cover and peered underneath. Mercédès joined him, looking under the pillows, feeling behind the horsehair mattress. She crawled under the bed, the dust clinging to her hair. Matteo checked the posts for words scratched into them. There was nothing.

'Any good?' said Mercédès, coming out again, rubbing under-bed grime out of her eyes.

He shook his head.

'Nothing under there either.' Her breath was coming faster, and she bit down hard on her lip. She looked to be trying not to cry.

His heart was sinking faster every second. Anton – sneering, scoffing Anton, his lip rolled up in ugly amusement as he leaned against the wall – was right. It was just a bed – a very large, very posh bed. You couldn't even eat it.

Suddenly there was a creaking noise in the next room. 'Oh, *Dieu!*' breathed Leo. 'The caretaker!'

They had forgotten to listen. And now, through the wall, they could hear slow, heavy footsteps. Leo darted into the enormous wardrobe, one door ajar, and Anton leaped behind the window curtains. Mercédès dived under the bed. Matteo shinned up one of the posts, and lay on the velvet roof of the bed, praying it would hold his weight.

The door swung open and a man trudged through. He was, Matteo saw, reading a newspaper as he went, and picking his nose with his spare hand. He flicked the snot on to the bed as he passed. Across the room, Matteo heard a small squeak of indignation from the wardrobe, quickly stifled: Leo.

The caretaker paused and sniffed. He looked left, right; then he took a step towards the wardrobe door.

The squeak came again, this time from under the bed; two small bursts, and a scrabble against wood, like claws on skirting board.

It was the squeak of a girl who spends a great deal of time with cats and their various rodent offerings.

The caretaker grunted. 'That had better be mice, not rats.' He sighed and stalked out, muttering, 'Poison in the basement.'

Matteo waited for his heart to stop beating in his ears. He counted to a hundred, and then a hundred again. He was about to climb down, when his whole body stiffened.

The entire top of the bed was embroidered with apples and pomegranates and pineapples, all painstakingly stitched in gold thread. It was dulled and worn with age, but still beautiful. But one of the pineapples had a vine attached, snaking from it, and the stitching was not in gold, but in silver.

'Wait!' He spoke barely above a nothing. 'Wait. *Fruitfully search*: fruit! There's a silver vine, here, on a pineapple.'

'Pineapples don't grow on vines,' said Anton.

'Yes, thank you, Monsieur Fruits-and-Vegetables, I have seen a pineapple before.'

He hadn't, actually, but that was not the point. His

heart was burning again with hope, because the snaking outline of the vine was, in fact, words: a cursive script, each letter sewn in minute silver stitches. It was the next clue. The words glittered in the dusty light:

David took paintbrush and conjured a scene
Of Napoleon crowned with his Josephine –
But ignore all the pomp as the crowds rhapsodise:
Find the X marks the spot, and follow his eyes.

And below it, in red stitching that barely showed against the red cloth, an extra couplet:

Go boldly, for boldness will pay,
And seek outside of the obvious way.

Anton's eyes were wide as tennis balls. His lips moved: he appeared to be memorising the words.

'A painting?' said Mercédès. 'It sounds like we have to find a painting of Napoleon?'

'There's only one place in Paris you go to look at paintings,' said Leo. 'The Louvre!'

* * *

89

The road back to Paris was dusty and dry, and lined with plane trees which seemed home to an unusual number of wasps. They stayed as much out of sight as possible, moving from tree to tree, but the cover was sparse, and it felt terribly exposed.

'We could ask someone, you know,' said Mercédès, as a four-horse carriage went galloping past, 'if they'd give us a lift.'

'What if they turned out to be Danglars? And anyway, I'd never get in a carriage with a stranger,' said Matteo. 'They could be thieves.'

Mercédès looked at him sideways through the corner of her eye. 'Aren't you a thief, though? More or less?'

'I,' said Matteo haughtily, 'am a taker-of-things-when-necessary. I'd never rob anyone.'

They stopped, three miles in, to bandage Mercédès' feet, which had blistered, and her fingers, which had been scraped raw in the climb. Neither had any spare cloth, so they used the soft leaves of the lime tree above, tied round with string.

'Does that help?'

'Yes. Quite a lot, actually. Why aren't you hurt too?'

He held his hands out – the palms were calloused so

thickly with scraping and healing and scraping again that he barely felt the scratches now. 'I have blister-proof hands.'

She smiled a quarter of a smile: just half of the left side. 'I think I'm getting tired of the blisters now. And of the always-alone. I want a ceiling, Matteo. I want a place to stay forever.'

Matteo, who did not want those things, who wanted sky and weather and just-him, nodded. 'Then we have to find you that.'

'Although,' she said and grinned, though the grin took effort, 'I'd miss having cat-teeth marks in all my fish.'

She looked like she would have said more, but there was the beat of a horse's hoofs around the corner coming towards them, and they moved off the road to the dry scrubby verge. And then Matteo felt his heart plunge, and he grabbed Mercédès by the wrist and pulled her down behind a tree.

He had recognised the horse before the rider: white, and beautiful, with unusually large hoofs. Danglars rode hard, lifting himself out of the saddle like a jockey, a whip in one hand and the reins in the other. Dust rose behind him in a cloud, and Mercédès took in a great gasp of horror and choked on it.

'He's going to Versailles,' said Matteo, when he had finished thumping Mercédès on the back. 'He must be.'

'But he's only got the first part of the clue! *There's silver vines amid the gold – Fruitfully search, for riches untold.* That could mean anything! How could he possibly know? Do you think he saw us get in the cart?'

Matteo raked through his memories. 'There … was a man, on the street corner by Sacré-Coeur, combing a horse … he looked familiar, but … I don't know!'

'Matteo! Will he solve the clue?'

Matteo set his jaw. 'No. Even if he knows that we went to Versailles, he still doesn't know the part about the *nodding head.* So he'll just have to search all seven hundred rooms. Good luck to him.'

Even so, Matteo felt his bones shiver, and he was suddenly cold. They quickened their pace back towards the city, cutting off the road and into the fields. It took far longer, and their clothes were covered with burrs and thorns, but they could not risk Danglars seeing them on his angry return journey.

CHAPTER EIGHT

L eo had given them careful instructions for visiting
the Louvre Museum.

'You should take a gift, because it's polite. Go after midnight. She likes to sleep in – she doesn't wake until one in
the morning.'

'What would she want, then?' said Matteo. 'For a present? I could steal her some steak?'

'No. She doesn't care about food. She only cares about
one thing.' And Leo had grinned. 'I can tell you exactly.'

Matteo knew the way to the British Ambassador's house.
They walked along the apex of the roofs on the Rue
Royale, pausing only for Matteo to snap off and pocket a
weathervane shaped like a cockerel.

'You know Paris well,' Mercédès said.

Matteo only nodded. It was true: and he did not believe in unnecessary modesty.

'You know, you never said where you lived before this – or really anything about who you are.'

'My secret.'

'Haven't you ever told anyone?'

'If I have a secret I need to tell, I whisper it in the ear of a stone statue. Ideally one of someone on a horse. And then it's just between the statue and me.'

'Does that actually work?'

'Yes.' And he jumped over a small alleyway and took off, running low on hands and feet. 'You should try it.'

They scraped the gilt off the little swirls on the upper balconies of the British Ambassador's house, and piled it into a fold of paper. It was dull work, and took a long time, because they had to keep ducking when the Ambassador's tiny child, dressed in what looked like a miniature admiral's uniform, came toddling to the window.

'Why does she want gold anyway?' said Matteo. He tasted a tiny bit of it. It was not delicious. 'This girl – this rooftopper – Valérie?'

'We'll see,' said Mercédès. 'Maybe she paints her nails with it.'

'That,' said Matteo, eating a little more, 'would be a deeply odd thing to do.'

They went slowly and cautiously to the Louvre. Matteo's nerves felt on fire; when they had to go down to the ground he checked and double-checked to see they were not followed.

The streets seemed deserted, except for a few women with enormous towering hairstyles making their way into a dance hall, and a few young men in evening dress, roaring with drunken laughter. Even so, Matteo's heart was pounding, and every time the white moonlight hit the window of a dark house as they passed by, he thought it was the face of Danglars.

The museum stood in the centre of its great square, hushed and dark and silent. It was one thirty, and even the seagulls were asleep, ranged along the top of the art gallery's dome.

They climbed in silence. It was a hard route, and Mercédès' breathing was unsteady. Matteo pulled himself upwards, and felt his muscles lengthen and contract. Up, up, and up – and all around him, the city sleeping, unaware that he was swarming up its proudest monuments.

The girl had been sitting cross-legged on the roof, next to an oil lamp turned very low, but as soon as their heads appeared over the top, she was on her feet. She nodded at them: wary, polite. It was a relief, Matteo thought, after Anton's sharp-edged welcome.

'I heard you might be coming. One of the pigeons brought a message from Leo.'

The girl had close-cropped hair, and deep, rich brown skin; and she was covered in stripes of colour – yellow chalk across one eyebrow, blue chalk inside her ear. Her nails were embedded with colours: orange, pink, green. And all around her, across the whole broad slate roof of the museum, there were drawings. Some – the largest – were intricately detailed, but most were just a few lines – the impression of movement, of flight. There were birds, butterflies, horses, people: but everything had wings. Even the boats had wings for sails.

'We were told you might like some gold,' said Mercédès. 'It was Leo's idea.' She handed it over, nervous, standing on one leg. The other girl took it and peered inside, and smiled.

'I'll put it on the Pegasus's wings,' she said. 'That will look fine.'

'And I brought you a weathervane,' said Matteo. 'They come in handy.' He crouched to study the drawings. He resisted the urge to touch them: their beauty was too delicate, he felt, to survive his touch. 'What happens when it rains?'

'I do more. I'm always here, so there's time. I almost never go down. I don't know why anyone would ever live at ground level.' She said *at ground level* the way other people might say *in the sewers*.

'What do you do, then, if the roofs are too far to jump, but you don't go down?'

Valérie grinned. She pointed to a wooden pole lying against the parapet. It was perhaps twice as tall as she was, and long and supple.

'It's made from solid ash wood,' she said. 'I whittled it myself. It took –' she counted on her fingers – 'seven weeks, four days, a hundred and eighteen splinters, three sliced fingertips and one close encounter with an owl.'

'An owl?'

'I took it from an ash tree in the Jardin des Plantes. The

97

owl was furious. It's better not to make an owl furious – they get very stabby. Here, I'll show you how it works.'

On one side of the buildings that make up the Louvre was the river, on the other a road, empty now, but wide enough for four carriages in the day. She ran along the length of the roof, gaining and gaining in speed. As she reached the end, she set the pole hard down on the rooftop, leaped, twisted, and soared two metres, two and a half – higher – three metres into the air, flying over the road, one hand still gripping the pole. She landed with an audible smack in a half-crouch, half-fall on the roof opposite. She rolled on to her left side, and stood up, rubbing her shoulder.

'Like that!' she called. 'It's more painful than is really ideal, but it does the work.'

'Doesn't anyone … see?'

'I only do it at night.' She grinned; she had a gap between her front teeth. 'And anyone who ever glimpses me just sees a flying shadow. They think they're drunk, or that it's maybe time to visit their eye doctor.'

She backed up along the roof, and vaulted back again. This time, Matteo saw it more clearly: how she twisted up and over the pole, feet above her head. She turned in mid-air and landed on her feet, stumbling only a little. 'That's what the landing's supposed to look like,' she said. 'It works about one time in twenty, I'd say.'

She put the pole back in its place. 'I once kicked a seagull,' she said, 'mid-flight. I was upside down. We both got a nasty shock. But it was its own fault for being out so late at night.'

'What happened to it?'

'I ate it. I have seagull most weeks. It tastes like greasy seawater. Xavier says it's not bad if you boil it, and then fry it, and have it with lots of salt. But then, if you boiled and then fried your shoe, it would probably taste nice enough too, so it's hardly an advertisement for seagulls. And I hate cooking, so I just shove it in the fire and hope for the best. But Xavier brings me proper food, sometimes.'

'Are we thinking of the same Xavier? The boy on the Arc de Triomphe?' Xavier had not struck Matteo as the madly generous sort.

'Mm. Pigeon, sometimes. Steak sandwiches, yesterday. I do him sketches of himself, in exchange, on top of the Arc: he doesn't have a mirror. But – you didn't come here to talk about food, or seagulls, or pole-vaulting. You came to talk about paintings. Leo said there's one in particular.'

Matteo recited the clue for her. 'So … a man called David, and a painting of Napoleon? Do you know it?'

'Of course I know the painting,' she said. 'I know all the paintings. Come! We go in via a skylight. It's pitifully easy. And you don't need to worry about the old night-watchman. He was in love with a rooftopper, once, when he was very young.'

'*What*? When?'

'Years ago. There have always been rooftoppers – ever since there were roofs. So he half knows I'm here, but he says nothing. Come on.'

There were a lot of eyes in an art gallery, Matteo thought. They walked past row after row of watchful faces: some were dancers, and some were kings, some beautiful, some extravagantly not so. One king looked like he had recently heard bad news and also had the misfortune to have a face made of mashed potato. They passed through a room of *Madonna and Childs*, and another of saints.

'All these paintings,' whispered Valérie. 'They were made by people with such care – every single stroke of paint had so much heart in it: so much human attention. A lot of people believed in the power of the saints they painted, you know? Now people come, and they shout and gossip and smoke their cigars and blow it in the faces of St Simeon and St Catherine, or leer at the girls who posed naked. So every night I go, in the dark. I hold the lantern up to them. I sit in front of them. I say, *Rest easy. I see you.*

'Here! This is the one! *The Coronation of Napoleon*, by Jacques-Louis David!'

The painting was not, itself, breathtaking, thought Matteo, although it was enormous, covering an entire wall of the gallery. It showed what looked to be a crowded hall, with golden walls and a throne, and a hundred people, all inclining their heads towards a man wearing a crown. A woman in an enormous red cloak knelt before him, and he was placing a crown on her head.

'That's the Empress Josephine, and Napoleon the Emperor.' Valérie struck her chest. 'The true hero of the people! *Liberté, égalité, fraternité* or death! Although, he did do quite a lot of murdering.'

'We're supposed to ignore all of them,' said Mercédès. 'The riddle said so: *But ignore all the pomp as the crowds rhapsodise: Find whose X marks the spot, and follow his eyes.* We need an X *marks the spot.*'

Matteo stepped close to the painting, his nose almost touching it. 'I don't see any Xs.'

'There's the cross that the priest is holding,' said Mercédès rather doubtfully. 'But it's got a Jesus on it. That doesn't seem right.'

'Wait!' said Matteo. 'Look! There, on the left!' The left of the painting showed an expanse of wall, and painted on to the wall was a small cross. Unlike the crucifix, each of the four branches were the same length. 'That could be an X!' he said. 'If you tilted your head a little!'

'And look, the wallpaper all around it is painted with spots!'

'X *marks the spot!*'

Directly under the cross, sixth from the left of the painting, stood a man: just a small painted head and shoulders, emerging from the crowd watching Napoleon. He, alone, was looking away from the Emperor; he was staring upwards.

'So … whatever his eyes are looking at is the location of the treasure?' said Valérie.

'Yes! Exactly that!'

'But what *is* he looking at?'

'Up, at any rate. Not at Napoleon!'

'At God, maybe?'

'It can't be that God has the diamonds. That's not how God works.'

'Well ... what then?'

'The ceiling?'

'Valérie – what building is this supposed to be?'

Valérie stared at him. 'I thought everyone knew that! Notre-Dame de Paris, of course! The cathedral.'

As she spoke, Danglars was almost close enough to smell them. His shoes barely made a noise as he moved closer to his goal. At his belt there was a gleam of metal, and he had the look of someone who had no intention of losing.

CHAPTER NINE

Matteo and Mercédès spoke in whispers as they made their way to the cathedral. It would have been twenty minutes' walk, but they did not walk: they roof-ran, on hands and feet, gripping brickwork and vaulting over skylights.

'We still don't know,' said Matteo as they clambered over the apex of a slate roof, 'where exactly to go, when we get to the cathedral. It could be glued to the ceiling, or inside the bells. I mean, a hundred-year-old painting … It's not particularly *specific*.'

'Then we'll try everywhere,' said Mercédès. She tested a piece of guttering before gingerly putting her foot on it. 'Even if it takes all night.'

Matteo nodded, and made the jump to the next rooftop. It was in bad condition, and the red roof tiles slipped under his hands and feet, so it was a minute before he realised she wasn't next to him. Mercédès had stopped short, one foot still on the guttering, and her mouth was open in shock. He ran back to her.

'Are you all right? Are you stuck?'

'I think maybe he *was* telling us!' she whispered. 'That final couplet, from the bed – the one that just sounds like a bit of poetic flourish:

Go boldly, for boldness will pay, And seek outside of the obvious way. What if he's saying *seek outside*? Outside, not inside!'

Matteo bit his lip. He nodded slowly. 'The roof.'

They had to drop down to ground level to cross the Pont Neuf, and Matteo scanned the streets over and over before he landed, barefoot, on the pavement.

'The good thing,' he said, 'is that roofs are on our side.'

Notre-Dame looked as though it was waiting for them. It was three in the morning when they reached it – three hours before sunrise. Its two great towers at the front were beginning to shade silver-grey as the night faded. Behind were the two long expanses of sloping roof, built in the shape of a cross, from the middle of which rose the tall needle spire. It is a spire all Parisians know and love, and use to find their way about the capital. All along the edges were the gargoyles, looking out with open mouths over the sleeping city.

'Ah. Oh. Right.' Mercédès looked up at the wall towering overhead, and her face changed shape and colour. 'It's … very high,' she said. 'It's the kind of height that comes with its own smell.'

'You don't have to come,' said Matteo. 'You can stay and keep watch, like before.'

Mercédès hesitated, then shook her head so hard her hair hit him in the face. 'If I come, we can search twice as fast. And every second we waste, Clotilde and Églantine are somewhere out there, in the wind and cold. Every second we waste, Danglars could be getting closer.'

'We don't have to go up the towers, at least,' said Matteo. 'We can go up the sides. And there're plenty of stone saints for handholds.'

It was only when they were standing atop the cathedral, balancing unsteadily on the slanted grey slate, that Matteo realised just how very enormous the rooftop of Notre-Dame actually was. His heart sank a little.

'OK. We search!' His attempt to sound optimistic came out more hyena-ish than he had meant it to, and he returned to his normal voice. 'I'll take the long length, you take the short one.'

He went along the gutter, running his hands through the leaves and dirt that had gathered there, squinting in the darkness. He swung himself down on to the wall of the cathedral, peering into the cupped hands of the saints set into the stonework. Half an hour became an hour. They met under the great black spire in the centre of the roof, and leaned against its moss-covered stone side.

'Nothing?' said Mercédès.

'Of course nothing.' Tiredness had seeped into his bones. It had been stupid, he thought, even for one second to entertain the dream that they might have found treasure. The real world was not a treasure kind of place.

'We don't give up!' said Mercédès. She jutted her jaw, and for a moment looked not unlike Napoleon himself. 'We must have been wrong about the *outside*. So we'll break in, and search inside.'

'How? Stained-glass windows don't open. And it's almost impossible to pick the lock on a church door. I know. I've tried.'

'Why?'

'I was going to eat the Communion bread.'

'Then we'll wait outside until it opens tomorrow, for matins, and we'll sneak in and search each of the four wings of the building, and then …' And then her whole face changed, her eyes opening so wide they seemed to take up half her face. 'The four sides of the building … Matteo! This rooftop – the cathedral – it's shaped like a cross! This, right here, the spire, is the centre of the X! X *marks the spot!*'

'What?' Matteo looked up. 'You think the treasure's at the top of the spire?' It was very thin and very high, and the moss that grew around the base of it looked thick and slippery. It was not a welcoming climb.

'Yes! This could be it, Matteo! Here – if we take off the moss …' Feverishly she began to scrape away the moss that had grown over the base of the dark-grey stone of the spire. And then her voice tailed off, because carved into the stone, curling around the base of the spire in ornately cursive letters, there were two lines.

You've come so far, my friends: prepare to gloat –
Now seize the day, and the gems, by the throat.

They stood staring at each other, each unconsciously clutching their throats.

'*Throat?* Does he mean … in the mouths of the saints? I checked all the saints on my side.'

Matteo screwed his eyes shut. He groped back into his own mind, trying to feel backwards to all the ideas and snippets he had heard, all the facts and all the jokes, through chimneys and windows and skylights.

Then he let out a gasp that rang like a bark through the night air. 'Throat! *Gargouille!* The mushroom professor – he said it was the old word for throat! *Gargouilles*, Mercédès! Gargoyles!'

He leaped to his feet and ran along the arc of stone-work that led to the nearest gargoyle. Paris shone beneath his feet. He went toe to heel – there was no reason to fall, he told himself, if he did not let himself think of falling. And then he realised, with a jolt: *I'm not afraid of falling any more.* Or, rather, of course he was: but he had spent so long up high, these last weeks, that he had become almost immune to its bite. It was as if, once you spent twenty-four hours a day up high, most of the fear wore off and you were left with only the beauty of the world around you. It was like wiping off mud to see the picture beneath.

He dropped to his hands and feet to approach the gargoyle. He would have to sit astride its neck to see its face properly. The gargoyle's head was covered in bird droppings, and its mouth was full of moss. Matteo pulled away the moss. Beyond it were tiny pebbles, and mud, set hard. Matteo scrabbled at it with his fingertips, wincing, hoping. His fingers broke through, and beyond the mud there was a fold of sacking. He pulled it away – and then his stomach dropped. It was as if he had fallen the thirty metres to the ground.

In the gargoyle's mouth was a diamond. It was the size of the top joint of his thumb, streaked with dirt, but there was no doubt about what it was. He gave a great whoop, and scrambled, one-handed, back on to the broad tiles of the roof.

'Mercédès! Look! Look!' And he dropped it into her small and soft and dirty palm, this shocking, shining thing.

You remember the first time you see a diamond. You remember how it caught at your chest. A glint of beauty, built under the earth, formed from dust and time.

Mercédès eyes were as wide as the night sky. 'Matteo! Oh my Lord, Matteo! We need to look in every single gargoyle!'

And Mercédès clambered, shaking, down on to one of the spears of stone that held up the next gargoyle, and reached into its mouth.

They made a pile, as the hour ticked by and as their gasps and cries shot through the night air to each other: a pile that glinted as it grew, red and green, blue and white. There was rough gold and smooth pearl; there were chunks of aquamarine, and tiny garnets as small as a grape pip. There were huge sapphires as large as marbles, gold-set emeralds, and a single ruby as big as a walnut. Each gargoyle gave forth a mouthful of hard-edged, shining bounty.

'Is that all of them?' said Mercédès at last.

Matteo looked upwards. 'Up there. At the top of the North and South Towers.' The gargoyles of the two towers, winged and horned and beaked, looked out over the city, keeping watch.

'Don't you think we have enough?' said Mercédès. 'It's already so much!'

But Matteo set his jaw. 'We can't let Danglars have them,' he said.

Immediately she understood. 'I'll take the South Tower, you take the North,' she said – and before he could ask her if she was sure, Mercédès was off, searching on the wall for handholds, her eyes grimly determined.

He scooped the piles of jewels into his pockets, and ran along the apex of the cathedral roof towards the North Tower. He climbed quickly, with a newly confident swing to his arms, a firmness to his knees. It felt fantastic and fantastical: he, the boy who people chased out of shops and halls, in pursuit of diamonds.

He scrambled over the edge of the tower, and landed softly on a dusty pile of coiled rope and some tools. Someone must have been repairing the stonework – some time ago, by the look of the dust on it. He leaned over the carved parapet and looked down. Mercédès was half-way up, hesitating over whether to grab on to an angel or what looked like it might be a carved pelican.

He was about to call out to her, to tell her to use the man's stone beard to the left of her, when a sudden movement caught his eye – and his entire body was swamped in ice. Climbing up the far side of the South Tower, a rope harness around his waist, his face tight and hungry, was Danglars.

Matteo ducked low. Danglars was moving twice as fast as Mercédès. He would be there when she came up over the top. It would be the work of a second to push her back over the edge.

Matteo's heart was beating with such thuds that it shook his whole body. He moved to swing down the side again, then stopped. He'd be too late if he tried to go down his tower and up the South.

'Mercédès!' he hissed. '*Mercédès!*' But she didn't hear, both eyes fixed on the wall in front of her.

Danglars advanced, wrapping his rope around the saints' heads as he went. Matteo's fear rose up in his mouth, and he swallowed it back. For a second he thought of what Xavier had said, about the calm that comes when you reach your most afraid. That was rubbish. His mind would not focus; his brain was shaking in his head.

His eye alighted on the rope and the tools. There was a pair of pliers, a broom, a grappling hook, some hammers, a screwdriver. An idea – a foolish, impossible one – took hold of him. He seized the grappling hook, and tied it to one end of the rope. He took aim, said a prayer to the gargoyles, and threw the hook with all the strength he had in his shaking arms.

Astonishingly, amazingly, it did exactly what he had planned. It flew in a high, lazy arc over the space between the towers, and landed on the South Tower with a gentle thud.

Danglars, winding the rope around St Francis, did not look up. He was very near the top now.

Matteo tugged at the rope slowly – so slowly that his bones creaked. The hook reached the balustrade. It caught against the edge. Matteo pulled, gently at first, then harder. The hook stayed in place. The blood in his head was roaring as he tied the other end of the rope as tight as he could around the ornate stone of his parapet, turning one of the screwdrivers in the knot to keep it taut.

He whispered, inaudible: 'Am I *really going to do this?*' He leaned over the parapet, and took the rope in his hands.

It was no good. His plan had been to swing himself, hand over hand, to the other side. But his hands were shaking too much.

Danglars' head appeared over the parapet on the other side. The man gave a crow of delight, and stopped to untangle himself from his harness. Mercédès was only a minute away from the top, her long hair whirling about her face in the wind.

Matteo's terror swelled up in him, up into his heart and head, into his mouth and nose. He let out a gasp of horror – and a sudden calm dropped over him like a blanket.

How rarely do we know exactly what to do? It had never happened to him before in his life. And here it was – as unlikely and impossible as it seemed.

Matteo climbed to stand on the parapet. He put one bare foot on the rope. It swayed under him, in exactly the way the branch of a tree swayed. It felt familiar. His heart was as smooth as a river in the sun as he stepped off on to the rope.

The rope was barely as thick as the top joint of his thumb. Three millimetres wrong to either side, he thought, and he was dead. But the rope, swaying under him, made sense, and he put one foot in front of the other, aligning it between his big and second toes, arms out to his sides.

He was five steps over the great drop into nothing when two things happened at once: Mercédès cleared the parapet, looked up, saw Matteo, and let out a cry; and Danglars spun round, one leg still in the rope harness, and gave a roar.

Matteo pushed his hands into his pockets and drew them out with a handful of jewels in each, arms out to the sides, a ruby sticking from his right fist, a chain of pearls trailing from his left.

'Danglars!' he called. 'Danglars! I have the jewels! If you take one step towards her – or towards me – I'll eat them! I'll start with the diamonds, and then I'll eat the sapphires and the rubies, and even if you kill me you'll never have them! Stay where you are!'

And the man did exactly that. Mercédès stood frozen in one corner of the tower, Danglars in another, as the boy on the tightrope moved towards them through the dawn, swaying, wobbling with a sudden desperate jerk but righting himself, his fingers clutched tight around a king's ransom worth of jewels.

Danglars' eyes were calculating distance and probabilities, and as Matteo was just a step away from the edge of the South Tower, he moved. He leaped, arms out, towards Matteo, aiming high, both hands out to grab at the boy's wrists.

But Mercédès moved first. In the corner of the South Tower was a pile of tools, even dustier than those on the North. She seized the broom, swung it about her like a fencing foil, and struck Danglars hard across the knuckles.

He whipped round, astonished. As he did so, Mercédès – the rooftopper who was afraid of heights, the girl who shivered in horror at the thought of an edge – scrambled up on to the balustrade. His mouth opened to roar as she launched herself with the agility and precision of a cat on to Danglars' shoulders. The two staggered, Mercédès clawing at Danglars' hair and ears, the man flailing at her – and then he tripped, and they both fell backwards against the stone.

Matteo clambered over the edge of the tower, stuffing the gems down deep into his pockets. He ran towards them, but there was a shout that made him halt. Danglars had straightened up, and Mercédès was backing away from the shining metal pistol in his hand.

'Thank you. That was all rather *fraught*. Let's keep things peaceable, shall we? Boy: are you listening?'

Matteo nodded. His teeth were gritted so tightly he could hear them creak.

'Good. I'm going to make this very simple. Take the jewels out of your pockets and put them in a pile, or I'll shoot her first and then you.'

Danglars smiled. How do you tell if a smile is real? It's an interesting question. This one was not. It was all teeth and fury.

Matteo's brain spun in search of an idea – and found none. He piled the gems in front of him, slowly, one by one.

'Faster.' Danglars approached, the gun pointing between Matteo's eyes. 'If I had my way, children would be put in boxes until they turn fourteen and are old enough to work. Very small boxes at first – and then larger, as they got older. One could post food in through holes when one felt like it. Children do nothing but create chaos.'

'I don't think that sounds very practical,' muttered Matteo. 'The children would break out of the boxes. You can't keep anyone shut down for too long.' But he spoke without thinking – his head was spinning. 'How did you solve the clues?'

'A tip-off,' said Danglars. Up close, he had one deep wrinkle across the width of his forehead – which suggested his eyebrows were often raised – and another, vertical, between his eyes. The tracks on his face had been made by disgust for the world. 'A young man called Anton was waiting for me at the entrance to Versailles. I did tell you, you know: do not underestimate what money can buy. And then I bribed the night-guard at the Louvre. That took a little time – I had to threaten to hunt down his family – but I got there eventually. '

The words knocked the wind out of Matteo's chest. But they had given new fire to Mercédès – she yelled, a sound with no words, in pure rage: she bent her knees, as if about to spring, but he lifted the gun again.

'The gun has two bullets. Two bullets, two children. I have exceptionally good aim. I take after my grandfather.'

'No!' said a voice behind them. There was a noise behind Matteo's head, of bare feet on stone. 'Not two children. Five.'

Valérie swung herself up and on to the top of the tower. In one hand she held the cockerel weathervane in front of her like a dagger. 'Xavier was keeping watch. He saw you coming this way.'

Xavier was right behind her, a knife in his belt, his hair in his eyes, and his face white with tension; and then Leo, out of breath and wild-eyed.

'I found out what Anton had done!' he said. Leo's large metal scissors stuck out from his pocket. 'I told the others.'

'Others?' said Matteo.

'Others!'

And there was a rustle and a hum and a hiss, as swarming up the sides of the cathedral came the tree-dwelling girls, their hair scraped back tight from faces which were set with fury. They held weapons in their hands, and they were not there to sing in the choir.

Danglars turned to stare at the hordes of children, his mouth open in a black hole of shock and horror and disgust. As Danglars turned, Matteo acted without thinking. He leaped at the pile of jewels, and ran across to the far side of the tower: the side that overlooked the river, black and hushed beneath them.

He jumped on to the parapet and called: 'Drop the gun or I'll throw them in the Seine!'

Danglars spun round, the gun still in hand. Matteo took one of the emeralds, closed his eyes, and hurled it over the tree next to the cathedral and into the river. He thought he could hear the almost inaudible splash it made as it disappeared under the surface.

Danglars dropped the gun. He gave a grunt that was not quite a word, and made a running snatch at Matteo's shoulder. Matteo ducked, threw out an arm to protect himself, and the diamond – the very first shining diamond he had found – flew out of his hand.

Danglars saw it. He roared and leaped after it, high and

flailing. He lunged, caught the jewel in his palm, gave a high crow of delight – felt his weight pull him to the left, grabbed at cold air, cried out again – was suspended for one moment in the nothing: and fell.

CHAPTER TEN

As the sun rose, anyone passing beneath the great oak in the gardens behind Notre-Dame would have heard an urgent and whispered conversation.

Matteo: 'And the old women? Where are they?'

Mercédès: 'Quickly, please!'

The redhead, Théa, licking at a deep cut along her calf, sliced against the stone of Notre-Dame: 'We found them on a bench, in the Tuilleries. *Ach!* This hurts.'

The brunette, Audra, peeling bark from the tree in long, careful strips: 'We invited them to live in the trees, but they said, "Arthritis".'

Devi, taking the bark and winding it in her swift brown fingers, softening it with spit: 'So they move from cafe to bar to restaurant, through the night.'

Ingrid, cutting the bark to size: 'And they sleep during the daylight.'

Phoebe, rubbing the bark with a paste, a mixture of onion and honey, taken from a small jar: 'They sleep upright, meercat-like.'

The twins Elisabeth and Brigitte, catching hold of Théa's ankles as she clambered past: 'On the benches.' 'Beneath us.'

Eugénie, miniature but strong, holding Théa still: 'We keep watch-guard.'

Ling, pressing the bark against Théa's wound: 'If anyone tried to hurt them, we'd apocalypse 'em.'

Anesu, tying the bark tight with a rope of plaited grass: 'We lullaby them. They maybe don't like it, but we do it anyway.'

Luci, offering her finger for the knot: 'I made a violin to play at them, out of strings and sticks. It sounds like a dying cat.'

Camille, testing the bark with her fingers, nodding: 'And anyone who comes too close, we squeeze a pigeon over them.'

Matteo: 'A dead one?'

Théa, twisting to stare: 'What good would that be? A living one! You squeeze it gently, just in the middle, between the wings, and the pigeon does a poo on the head below.'

Tatenda, grinning: 'So they always have the bench to themselves.'

And Audra, her voice serious: 'But they don't have the money for the cafes any more. So Madame Églantine is going to sell her violin: and after that ...' The leaves rustled as the girls shook their heads in unison. 'So we need to move fleet-swift.'

Sitting on a bench under a chestnut tree, Clotilde was trying to plait her hair, but the wind was strong, and her hands had taken to shaking. Frustrated, she tried to use the end of the braid to wipe away the tears before Églantine saw them – but hair does not work on tears or snot or sweat, as Matteo could have told her.

Églantine sat next to her on the bench. A balding man with a paunch stood over her. He held her violin case in one hand, and with the other he laid a piece of paper in front of her. It was headed: *Maker and Seller of Stringed Instruments, 16 Rue Charlemagne.*

'Just sign here, Madame,' he said.

Églantine lifted her chin so high it was pointing at a spot about six inches below the treetops. Her wrinkled old neck ached with the effort. She picked up the pen, then laid it down in her lap again.

The man cleared his throat. 'As quick as you can, Madame. I have other clients I must see.'

Églantine picked up the pen again – and there was a crash, and out of the tree above them dropped what looked like a ball of leaves and dust.

It had arms and legs and huge, staring eyes, and a face so shining you could have lit a city from it.

'Stop! Stop! Madame Clotilde! Madame Églantine! *Everything is changed!*'

And the child – a girl child – a child the same shape as the shadows they had sometimes seen through the window – a child of the kind they would have dreamed of, if they had been permitted to have that kind of dream – dropped to a crouch in front of them and turned out her pockets.

'They're yours!' said the child. 'The clue was yours, and his house was yours, so the jewels are yours. For you! I swear I didn't steal them. I promise!'

And a cascade of jewels fell on to their laps: gold, diamonds, rubies, shining on their woollen skirts.

It was several moments before anyone could say anything – and then there was so much shouting and explaining and *it-can't-be*-ing that it was many hours before everything was clear. We are not good, as a human species, at accepting that extraordinary things do sometimes happen.

Sometimes it doesn't come right. Sometimes – perhaps more often – nobody comes, and you make what you can from what is left. You weather it, as millions have done and will continue to do.

But sometimes a girl with eyes like a victory parade bursts in and calls your name. Our world has both.

CHAPTER ELEVEN

There had, of course, to be a feast.

It began with a fire. They met on top of the church of Sacré-Coeur, and Xavier, his ear to the wind, knew the exact right moment: the point when the voices of the city had fallen silent enough for the fire to be lit.

Mercédès – dressed in one of Leo's creations, a pair of sea-green shorts stitched to a red top – came, teeth gritted, over the side. 'This is the only thing I won't miss when I go – the edges.'

Clotilde and Églantine were moving to the sea, and Mercédès was going with them. 'We'll sing at the sea,' she had said, when she had told Matteo, 'and the sea will sing back.'

'It won't, you know,' said Matteo. 'The sea doesn't. I meant to mention it before, but it seemed impolite at the time.'

Mercédès laughed. 'Won't you come, anyway? Please?'

But they had both known he would not.

Now Valérie helped Mercédès to her feet. 'Remember – it's just a height!' she said. 'It's not going to move, or bite you – you're the one with the control, not it.'

'Fine! I know that's technically true, but will you tell that to my heart and lungs and stomach? Because they've taken a vote and they don't believe you.'

She laid her offering down with care – an entire wheel of cheese, sweet and fresh and nutty, as large around as a football. 'This is from Clotilde and Églantine.' Mercédès' hair was newly washed, and her face shone with the look of someone who is freshly cherished.

'You need to have a theme, for a feast,' Xavier had said, and Matteo had suggested it: 'Things you've never really got enough of'. There were grapes – tiny green ones, and pinkish red ones that you could see the light through, and six bunches of a dark purple that was almost black. The tree-dwellers brought the bunches tied on to strings and slung round their necks like scarves, shedding as they went.

'Did you grow them?' asked Mercédès, impressed, and was met with peals of laughter.

'We snatch-fled them,' said the smallest. 'But don't be cross. The shop-man won't mind. He didn't even notice they were gone – we're really *very* good at the taking.'

They also brought an extremely long-legged boy named Gérard. 'He lives in the oak by the Academy of Music, but it fell down three nights ago. He's looking for somewhere to live.' Gérard's trousers were too short, and he seemed to be built largely of ankle and wrist. He had brought chocolate cake, broken into six pieces to better fit in his pockets. He looked around the rooftop with approving eyes. 'I had never thought,' he said, 'of living on a church.'

From Matteo, his pockets full of coins from Clotilde, there was what looked like the entire window display of a bakery. He laid them out on the stone: eclairs with vanilla cream, six brioches filled with chocolate custard, a pyramid of strawberry tarts and a dozen yellow cakes topped with candied cherries. Xavier brought snails roasted with garlic, which Matteo privately thought disgusting, but which the tree-dwellers ate with ferocious passion.

Valérie brought a bowl of whipped cream. 'I hate cooking. But I don't mind hitting things with a stick. I whisked it with a willow bough.'

Leo did not bring food. He brought a large sack, and emptied it on to the slate in a great flash of colour.

The tree-dwellers fell on the clothes. There was an eruption of arguing – and then there they stood, shining. Some wore sun-yellow trousers and golden waistcoats, some in green skirts embroidered with crowns and purple jackets embroidered with apples, one in a rose velvet dress, cut short in the sleeve and high in the neck, flashing around her knees as she ran like a salutation to the day.

Leo moved among them, his long, careful fingers stitching here, pinning there. 'That's perfect, that's exactly as it should be,' he would say, or, to Théa, 'No, that colour isn't as good to you as you deserve – here! Sea-green!' And the girl flushed with pleasure, beneath her tangled twig-filled hair. Audra turned a cartwheel in her new clothes: deep-blue trousers and a loose sky-blue shirt that flapped about her elbows as she twisted across the skyline.

Leo looked at them, his head slightly cocked, lips pursed. He turned to the others. 'What I wanted,' he said, 'was for them to look like they chopped a rainbow down from the sky, and cut it into pieces, and put it on. What do you think?'

'That is exactly what they look like,' said Xavier.

'*Exactly* like,' said Mercédès.

'Then I'm pleased.' But his smile was less wide than it had been when they had met him in the sun at Versailles.

They toasted bread over the fire, and balanced the cheese on top, and ate it with the taste of woodsmoke still rich on it. They ate from both fists at once – without worrying about a little cream on one's chin or chocolate on one's collarbone. They ate to celebrate, because there are certain foods that taste of pure celebration. They ate to say: *These are the lives that we have been dealt, and we will make our days into good ones.*

Matteo was the last to stop eating, but eventually even he began to feel that anything he put into his mouth might have to come out again immediately, one way or another. Valérie took chalk from her pocket, cleared the dust and moss from a spot in the slate, and drew them – Matteo, Mercédès, Xavier, Leo.

Anton was missing. Leo went red every time his brother's name was mentioned. When he had returned to the roof at Versailles, he had found Anton gone. They had tried to persuade Leo to move in with the tree-girls, or to find a new rooftop in town, but he refused. 'He's my brother. I have to be there, just in case he comes back. It's just … it's how it is.'

'We'll come and visit,' said Théa. 'And if he's there, we'll wallop-smash him.'

'And then we'll stop, and bandage him up,' said Devi. 'Because you love him.'

'I won't,' said Théa.

Valérie sharpened her chalk on the stone, and kept drawing. It was almost impossible to draw the tree-girls – they wouldn't stop moving: one kept trying (and failing) to climb one of the three vast white domes of the church – but there they were, in a few swift lines, arms and legs and hair.

'The rain will take it eventually,' she said. 'But until then. That's us.'

Mercédès and Matteo had met for one last time on the Cristo roof. They smoked a cod inside the chimney, and ate it with fried potatoes.

The cats clustered around them. 'I'm taking the tabby,' said Mercédès, 'and the black kitten, and the mangy grey. But the rest are Paris cats – they won't want to come.'

'You want me to look after them?'

'No! They don't need looking after. They used to feed

me, not the other way around. But, if you see them about, will you bow?'

Matteo pulled a face. 'Maybe. I don't promise things.'

'They appreciate it. They're like everything, you know – they just want you to notice they're there.'

Matteo ate more cod with his fingers. They had cooked it well, and it was barely disgusting at all. He half shrugged and half nodded, and said nothing.

Years later, when Matteo was tall as a doorway and with a handsome collection of scars, others would wonder why he always bowed when greeted by a cat.

It was some time afterwards that Xavier came to find Matteo. It took him a while – Matteo was searching for his new home. The Opera House, he had decided, had too many nymphs. He liked the look of the Law Courts: the building was high, and flat, and there were flags flying from the sides. He could make those flags into sheets, he thought. If he sewed them with feathers, they would be as thick and warm as blankets.

Xavier crouched down in the centre of the roof and looked out over the city. 'Matteo,' he said. 'I'm going.'

Matteo was startled enough to look up from pacing out the space of the rooftop, planning the glorious feather bed he would make. 'What? Where?'

Xavier shrugged magnificently: his shoulders and eyes and eyebrows and hands all went up and down together. 'Everywhere! Maybe the Brihadisvara Temple. Maybe the Sistine Chapel. I don't know. I like the idea of Buckingham Palace.'

'How will you get there? Stow away?'

'Exactly! So this is me saying goodbye,' said Xavier. He strode to the edge of the roof, raised one hand in salute, and lined his toes up, ready to jump.

'But – wait! Who's going to keep watch over the city, if you go? Who's going to notice it? Who's going to collect its secrets?'

Xavier grinned. 'I would have thought that was obvious. You, of course.'

'Me?' Matteo felt the rooftop shift under him, tilting under his toes. 'But I don't know how!'

'You have eyes that know how to look at things. You fought, when you saw two old women out on the street. Eyes, and heart – that's all it is.' And without another word, he stepped off the edge of the roof and landed in a crouch on the window sill two metres below.

Matteo leaned over the edge of the roof, flat on his stomach, and called down. 'Xavier?'

'What? I was trying to make a dramatic exit, Matteo.'

'One last thing!'

'Hurry up, then.' He jumped another three metres down, to the next window sill, landing on one foot.

'There's one jewel left – a ruby. Mercédès gave it to me when she left for the sea, but I wouldn't know what to do with a ruby. I'd spend all my time worrying people were going to steal it, or that it was going to fall out of my pocket. But … I've got a plan.' And, with the blood rushing to his eyeballs, hanging half upside down, he told Xavier what he had been plotting.

Xavier's eyes lit up. 'Yes! Good. I like that. I'll race you there.' And he swung on to the drainpipe, and down and away.

Matteo pulled off his boots and ran. Not, as he always had before, the swift scrambling on hands and feet, but a real run – leaping over moonlit nothing, landing on slate, his heart swelling until it felt like it would push everything else out of the way, kidneys and stomach and lungs crushed to the edges, and he was nothing but his own beating heart.

It is possible to feel homesick for a place you have never been and cannot describe. Matteo, without knowing, had spent his life homesick for the sky, and he had come home to it, and he flew through it: running, leaping, skystepping.

Somewhere, up high above the bustle of Paris, among the chimney pots and gargoyles, there is hidden a ruby the size of a walnut. Nobody has found it yet.

But Matteo left a clue, etched into the stone on top of Notre-Dame's South Tower. And it is copied here, for anyone feeling brave:

Go to the city's tallest point,
And climb to the tip of the iron joint.
It's waiting, tied tight, the size of an eyeful:
It's less than a fortune – but more than a trifle.

AUTHOR'S NOTE

I often get asked about how much of my stories is real: so, here are some things that are true. The painting *The Coronation of Napoleon* by Jacques-Louis David is a very real one and hangs on a wall of the Louvre, and there really is one young man in it looking upwards, sixth from the left. There really are more than two thousand windows in Versailles, and it really is the kind of beautiful that blows your hair back, and the Sun King did have a bed canopy in red, silver and gold, and boiled eggs for dessert. You really can string a tightrope between the two towers of Notre-Dame de Paris: a man called Philippe Petit did exactly that, in 1971. I do not know if, were you to bow at enough cats, one of them would bring you fish for your dinner, but I think it is worth trying.

ABOUT THE AUTHOR

Katherine Rundell is the bestselling author of five children's novels and has won the Costa Children's Book Award, the Blue Peter Book Award and the Waterstones Children's Book Prize amongst many others. Her novels are now published in more than thirty countries. Katherine spent her childhood in Zimbabwe and Belgium before taking her degree at the University of Oxford and becoming a Fellow of All Souls College. As well as writing, she studies Renaissance literature at Oxford University and goes climbing across rooftops, secretly, late at night.

Books to feed the imagination.
Go on an adventure with

KATHERINE RUNDELL

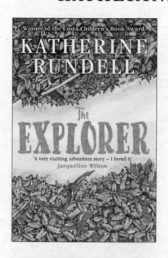

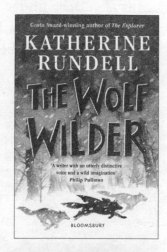

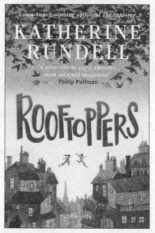

When Fionn Boyle sets foot on
Arranmore Island, it begins to stir beneath
his feet. Deep underground, someone has
been waiting for Fionn, and soon a
new Storm Keeper will rise …

Read on for a gripping extract from the first

book in this magical, spellbinding trilogy …

AVAILABLE NOW

THE WOMAN WHO FOUGHT THE SEA

Just after midnight, Fionn sat bolt upright in bed with a scream trapped in his throat. He wiped his brow, his gaze travelling the length of the shoebox he and Tara were sharing. Moonlight seeped in through a crack in the curtains, casting strange shadows across the walls.

Tara sighed and turned over in her bed. Fionn knew she hadn't found the enchanted Sea Cave earlier, but whatever she did get up to had kept her away for most of the day.

We're going to try again tomorrow. That's the thing about adventures, Fionny. They take a bit of time.

This time, Fionn hadn't asked if he could go with her.

He knew she would say no. She was still stewing about the doll thing. Plus, the fact remained: he was afraid of the sea. And now everyone knew it.

It needled him that Tara was right. He was not brave. He didn't know how to be brave. Whenever he watched *The Lord of the Rings*, he imagined himself as a lone rider galloping away from a battle while all the other characters were marching into it. When everyone else was in Helm's Deep, he'd be back in the Shire, making a sandwich.

Even so, he couldn't stop thinking of the Sea Cave. If there really was a wish hidden somewhere on the island, would he have enough courage to go and get it? What if he met the same fate as his father? He had fallen asleep imagining himself crawling inside it, through seaweed and seafoam, shouting his wish at the top of his lungs. It was only when the dream turned to visions of a cave swallowing him up like a mouth, that he lurched wide-eyed from his sleep.

He slipped out of bed and into the hallway, trailing his fingers along the shelves of candles as his grandfather's snores echoed through the little cottage.

In the sitting room, Fionn was surprised to find the giant candle still blazing on the mantelpiece. It was a fire hazard, surely, and yet, considering the way the wind was squeezing itself through the cracks in the walls and howling down the chimney like a banshee, the candle was probably the least of this place's problems. He watched the flame for longer than he intended to. The sea settled in the air around him, and Fionn opened his mouth and tasted a storm on his tongue.

His gaze was drawn to a shelf tucked away in the corner of the room, where a small, dark blue candle was peeking out from behind a lopsided wax snowflake. It was round and squat, like a piece of fruit, with a silver thread zigzagging through the centre.

The label glinted at him in the dimness.

Evelyn, it said.

Fionn climbed on to his grandfather's chair and plucked the candle from the shelf. Why would he name a candle after his mother? And why was it hidden away in the furthest corner of the cottage?

He traced the silver streak with the pad of his thumb as he lifted the wick to his nose. There was no smell. He hopped off the chair and found a box of matches at the end of the mantelpiece. He lit the wick and the flame sparked with a faint *whoosh*. The scent enveloped him: hurried strides across damp earth, grass collecting between toes, the bite of an unforgiving wind. And there beneath the rest of it, two different kinds of salt: warm teardrops in a freezing ocean.

What on earth ... ?

Fionn held the burning candle in his hand until his curiosity yawned and stretched itself into action. A rogue breeze had slipped underneath the front door and was curling around him.

It pressed itself against his back.

Walk, something inside him said.

He waded out into the night.

This way.

The air shimmered as he pushed through it, the wind shoving harder until he was running so fast his feet were barely touching the ground. The flowers shrank into the earth around him and the grass grew until it brushed his ankles. He didn't notice his bare feet scraping on the rough earth, or the cold seeping through his pyjama bottoms. He followed the moon with the flame in his hand and the wind at his back as the island swept by him.

He stumbled past sleepy houses and little cars, the secondary school and the corner shop and the pub.

The island was beautiful dappled in moonlight. It looked like a black and white painting, punctured with amber flecks, where stragglers were still awake, reading or watching television. They winked in and out as Arranmore rose and disappeared above him, and a new one crept up from the ground.

When the wind finally settled, Fionn hovered on the edge of the beach and watched the sea get angry. The waves swelled, spraying the pier with foam as thunder rumbled through storm clouds so dark they ate the stars.

There was a girl standing in the middle of the sea. The fractured moonlight danced on the crown of her head, and dark hair tumbled down her back, tangling and swaying like ropes.

Fionn hopped over the wall and ran on to the beach, panic guttering in his throat.

'Tara!'

The wind took the name from him and gobbled it up.

'Tara!' She was so far in, he didn't know if she could wade back out again. Not with the waves tugging at her elbows. She started flailing her arms, like she was trying to beat up the sea with her fists. The clouds swirled lower, static crackling along their underbellies as the thunder growled like an angry bear.

Fionn raced to the edge of the beach, where it curved into the sea in a peninsula. The candle was still clamped in his fist, the flame fighting the wind the way his sister was fighting the sea. The wax was melting over his knuckles but he didn't feel it.

When he reached the end of the peninsula, the waves dipped and Fionn saw a bump protruding from the girl's stomach.

He looked at her face. More closely, this time.

'Mam?' This time, the storm didn't steal the name. It spluttered out all on its own.

Fionn's mother was screaming at the sea. The sky was roaring back.

'Mam!' Fionn waved the candle in the air, like a flare. 'Mam! Come back!'

A wave crashed against her and she fell backwards, a hand cupping her swollen belly. She scrambled to get back up but another one washed over her head, burying her from view.

Fionn launched himself into the water. The waves spat in his eyes and tangled salt in his hair, pushing him back to shore. The harder he tried to get to his mother, the harder the ocean fought back.

And then from the darkness came a flash of pale skin and long limbs. Fionn's grandfather appeared as if from nowhere, hurtling across the strand like an Olympic athlete and flinging himself into the sea head first.

He resurfaced ten strides later, his bald head shiny with droplets. He seemed so much younger now, so agile and fearless. The wind didn't steal his warnings the way they had taken Fionn's – they tornadoed round and round, as loud and stubborn as a ship's horn.

'Evelyn!' He yelled, his arm looping around her as he tugged her backwards. 'Come out of there before you drown, Evie!'

Fionn tried to wade towards them but the sea danced around him in a prison of salt and brine until he lost his balance. He dropped the candle and the flame went out.

The island inhaled.

Fionn's grandfather disappeared and took his mother with him. The tide sank and the clouds evaporated into a star-laden night. Without the clash and clamour of a troubled sky, Fionn could hear his heartbeat in his ears.

He remembered to be afraid, and once he did, the fear climbed down his throat and stole his breath.

He was in the sea! And the sea was going to drown him! He stumbled backwards and tripped on a rock, his body twisting as he fell. He landed face first in the ocean and inhaled a lungful of seawater. A wave rolled over him. And then another.

Come out of there before you drown, Fionn!

It wasn't his grandfather's voice now; it was his own.

Fionn dragged himself from the water, spluttering and vomiting on to the sand. He crouched there, shaking and panting, until the stars in his vision winked out. Then he rolled on to his back and stared out at the empty sea. It was calmer than he had ever seen it, the sky above a star-speckled obsidian.

He got to his feet. He had only been underneath the water for a few seconds, but the sea had made the most of it. He was sopping wet from head to toe. Crystals of salt were stuck to his eyelashes and streaks of seaweed had woven themselves into his hair.

He trudged home, wincing from the pain in his feet.

Slowly, slowly, the world reset itself.

He did his best not to think about the island as it

watched him go by. What it had taken from his family all those years ago. Why his mother had waded into the sea and screamed at it like that.

Where was she now? Was she there, or here?

Where was his grandfather? Swimming underneath the tide like a fish or at home in bed where Fionn had left him?

Where am I?

In the cottage, Fionn peeled off his wet pyjamas and changed into new ones. He dried his hair with a tea towel in the little hallway outside his grandfather's bedroom, listening to the steady rise and fall of his snores. How could he have been in two places at once? Fionn couldn't wrap his tired brain around it.

In the kitchen, he made himself a cup of tea, then took it through to the sitting room where he watched the candle on the mantelpiece with a new sliver of mistrust. Why was it lit? And what was it doing to him? He peered around the dusky room, half expecting a ghost to unfold from the patchwork chair. It was stupid to leave a candle burning at night. Hadn't anyone ever told his grandfather that?

This thing could kill us all.

Fionn set his mug down.

Then he stood in front of the fireplace and blew the candle out.

It exhaled like a sleeping giant and pushed a breeze through the cottage that rattled the windowpanes. Fionn felt it on his ankles as he sank into his grandfather's chair.

There. That's better.

Exhaustion swept over him as the tea settled into his bones. Sleep dragged him to a dark place, where he forgot his name and the island along with it, until –

'HELP ME!'

Fionn jerked awake to the sound of his grandfather shouting the walls down, his fingers scrabbling to light the candle on the mantelpiece. Spittle was gathering at the sides of his mouth and his breath was stuttering out of him in laboured gasps.

'WHAT HAVE YOU DONE!' he shouted, his fingers slipping and sliding as another match snapped in half.

Fionn sprang to his feet and grabbed the matches from his grandfather's shaking hands. He lit the candle on the first strike. The flame hissed as it climbed towards the ceiling, raging and thrashing as if it was angry with him for blowing it out. The darkness broke apart and flecks of dust floated around Fionn's surprised face.

He shuffled backwards. He was afraid of his grandfather, wild-eyed and unkempt in his mismatched pyjamas. He was so much frailer than the man Fionn had seen in the ocean, dipping and diving like a fish. He towered over him now, the light bleeding back into his eyes as he took Fionn by the shoulders and pulled him close.

'I will tell you this once and once only, lad. As long as you live here in this house, as long as you live on this island, as long as you draw breath and pump blood around your body, you are never, *ever*, to touch that candle again.' He brought his nose right up to Fionn's, two sides of the same coin staring into the same deep blue eyes. 'Do you understand?'

Fionn could feel his pulse in the tips of his ears. 'I understand.'

His grandfather turned and stalked out of the room like a storm cloud, his footsteps thundering back to his bedroom where he slammed the door behind him. Fionn froze in the middle of the sitting room, surrounded by hundreds of candles that peered over him judgementally.

His sister stood across from him in her Hogwarts pyjamas, her arms folded across her chest. 'I told you never to touch that candle, Fionny.'

Fionn wanted to launch himself across the room and shake her and shake her and shake her until all of her meanness fell out.

He swallowed the quiver in his throat. 'No, you didn't.'

'Oh,' she said, shrugging her way back into the darkness. 'Well, I meant to.'

'You didn't tell me anything!' Fionn called after her, but she was already gone.

In the seething silence, Fionn's mind started to whirr. The truth was unavoidable now – he had seen it. He had *lived* it. Arranmore was full of secrets.

The island was full of impossibility.

Be brave.

The island had magic.

This is your adventure.

And he was going to find a way to use it.

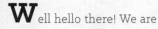

Well hello there! We are

Overjoyed that you have joined our celebration of

Reading books and sharing stories, because we

Love bringing books to you.

Did you know, we are a charity dedicated to celebrating the

Brilliance of reading for pleasure for everyone, everywhere?

Our mission is to help you discover brand new stories and

Open your mind to exciting worlds and characters, from

Kings and queens to wizards and pirates to animals and adventurers and so many more. We couldn't

Do it without all the amazing authors and illustrators, booksellers and bookshops, publishers, schools and libraries out there –

And most importantly, we couldn't do it all without . . .

You!

Rob Biddulph

From breakfast to bedtime, there's always time to discover and share stories together. You can . . .

1 Take a trip to your local bookshop

Brimming with brilliant books and helpful booksellers to share awesome reading recommendations, you can also enjoy booky events with your favourite authors and illustrators.

Find your local bookshop:
booksellers.org.uk/bookshopsearch

2 Join your local library

That wonderful place where the hugest selection of books you could ever want to read awaits – and you can borrow them for FREE! Plus expert advice and fantastic free family reading events.

Find your local library:
gov.uk/local-library-services/

3 Check out the World Book Day website

Looking for reading tips, advice and inspiration? There is so much to discover at **worldbookday.com**, packed with fun activities, audiobooks, videos, competitions and all the latest book news galore.

Rob Biddulph